W9-BUF-846

Additional Acclaim for
The Faithful Narrative of a Pastor's Disappearance

"Anastas is not merely clever but also brilliant and perceptive . . . flawless . . . *Faithful Narrative* is the rare kind of book that compels its readers to underline certain passages and read them aloud to friends."
—*Hartford Courant*

"Hands down the best novel of the year is Benjamin Anastas's *The Faithful Narrative of a Pastor's Disappearance*, and I will not stand corrected."
—Daniel Handler, *Newsday*

"[A] starkly written tale of suspicion and doubt." —*Baltimore Sun*

"[*The Faithful Narrative of a Pastor's Disappearance*] breathes a quiet faith. And it's the best kind of faith, one that's loving, inclusive, and abundantly aware of shared human foibles."
—Mark Luce, *The Washington Post Book World*

"Mr. Anastas can write. . . . [He] captures angst in the suburbs, detailing materialism gone haywire, and he peoples his village with entertaining characters. . . . Much of the book is witty, and much is sad, filled with a lonely yearning for grace." —*Gotham*

"Writing with the same panache he brought to his clever first novel, Anastas again proves himself a smart literary voice. . . . [*The Faithful Narrative of a Pastor's Disappearance*] sparkles with dry wit and a generous understanding of human complexities."
—*Publishers Weekly*

"Charming . . . displays the writer in full literary bloom . . . It is an amiably rambling, deeply spiritual, energetically written novel that alternates between pointed, hilarious satire and aching, soulful sadness." —*The Commercial Appeal*

"A real generosity and tenderness." —*The New York Observer*

"[A] wonderfully crafted, emotionally resonant novel . . . With its vexed Puritan heritage, New England has long been ready fodder for chaffing, and *The Faithful Narrative*, whose hypocrisies and subtle ironies delicately adhere to the text like gold leaf, is no less a study in social satire."

—*The Bloomsbury Review*

"This is that rare novel that can get away with putting the ending at the beginning . . . Anastas's gifts for description and characterization make this work a literary as well as a satirical masterpiece."

—*Salt Lake City Deseret News*

The Faithful Narrative

of a

Pastor's Disappearance

Also by Benjamin Anastas

An Underachiever's Diary

The Faithful Narrative

of a

Pastor's Disappearance

A Novel

Benjamin Anastas

Picador USA

Farrar, Straus and Giroux

New York

www.picadorusa.com

Picador® is a U.S. registered trademark and is used by Farrar, Straus and Giroux under license from Pan Books Limited.

For information on Picador USA Reading Group Guides, as well as ordering, please contact the Trade Marketing department at St. Martin's Press.
Phone: 1-800-221-7945 extension 763
Fax: 212-677-7456
E-mail: trademarketing@stmartins.com

Library of Congress Cataloging-in-Publication Data

Anastas, Benjamin.
    The faithful narrative of a pastor's disappearance / Benjamin Anastas.
        p. cm.
    ISBN 0-312-42068-4
    1. Afro-American clergy—Fiction. 2. Missing persons—Fiction.
3. Massachusetts—Fiction. I. Title.

PS3551.N257 F3 2001
813'.54—dc21   00-045609

First published in the United States by Farrar, Straus and Giroux

First Picador USA Edition: May 2002

10 9 8 7 6 5 4 3 2 1

There is nothing that the devil seems to make so great a handle of, as a melancholy humor; unless it be a real corruption of the heart.

—Jonathan Edwards

First Part

 The founding member of the Monday Reflection Group noticed first, arriving at the church to find the pastor's driveway empty and the curtains in the parsonage still drawn, but she knew nothing of his sudden and astonishing disappearance, not yet, only that the Reverend Thomas Mosher, well-liked minister of the Pilgrims' Congregational Church ("An Historic Church with a Modern Message" they included below their name in all the literature) in W———, Massachusetts, spiritual mentor to his well-heeled but undeniably eccentric congregants, author of competent—if sometimes esoteric—Sunday sermons heavy on the Book of Psalms, culminating in his very last one, "The Shapes of Love," which had veered away from the usual Easter Cycle to explore the possibility that God is an "infinite sphere," an idea that had bored some members of the church *dumb* and had seemed to others inappropriate for a Trinitarian; eligible bachelor rumored to have carried on an affair with a married woman in the church, Bethany Caruso (née Coleman), the mother of a preteen son and pious daughter widely considered *angelic*, if, at times, unusually frank when speaking to adults,

and prone to disruptive behavior during Sunday school, the product, many believed, of Bethany's frequent separations from her husband (not a regular churchgoer), making her, already envied for her smoldering good looks and close relationship with the pastor, the object of persistent disapproval, despite the fact that an adulterous tryst between the two had never been confirmed, and the Reverend Mosher, according to the local women who openly pursued him—Sadie Maxwell, flashy owner of the town's leather boutique; twice-divorced Alessandra Palacios y Rio, self-styled socialite and beneficiary of a Hollywood divorce settlement—showed no interest in matters of the flesh, possessing, as he did, an awkward bearing in the world of men and women, little sense for the subtleties of flirtation and its deeper second step, seduction; truth be told, the Reverend Mosher seemed comfortable only at the pulpit, draped in his black Geneva gown and elevated *slightly* above his audience, able to communicate with an ease that usually escaped him, projecting authority with his lovely voice (they all agreed that, with their eyes closed during the morning prayers, his intonation could often be *transporting*), while in life he was acutely absentminded, a chronic mumbler, famous for calling members of the church by the wrong name, as well as accident-prone (how many times had he driven his car, the unfortunately named Ford Probe, off the road? The product of relentless dreaming), known for his inept pitching in church league softball, and sloppy housekeeping, according to the Thursday Housekeepers, who grew so tired of scrubbing down the parsonage they pooled their resources and hired a cleaning woman; no, the Reverend Mosher was not like the dull and energetic middle managers who had lately moved to town for a short commute and joined the congregation out of some *imagined duty*, who talked too loud among themselves and, but for a few opening minutes, paid little attention to his painstakingly prepared sermons, although there were notable exceptions, troubled men who had no choice but to display their depth, like high-strung Carlo Wagner, a physicist with a wide repertoire of nervous tics (clearing his throat, touching his glasses, pinching the end of his nose, scratching his ear with an index finger, and twitching, all in no particular order), or Ed Brooks, a school administrator who was obviously manic-depressive, but refused his wife's attempts to have him seek counseling and—this was her ardent hope, expressed in weekly talks with the Reverend Mosher—a prescription for antidepressants, no longer a stigma in the community, or even a topic of gossip and/or debate, quite the opposite: Paxil and Zoloft had long since entered the local vocabulary, and stood, now, for happiness and hope, as if a tablet could ever contain these illusory states of being, reinventing the founding principles of W———, Massachusetts, as well as of every other place in the New World chosen by displaced men and women for settlement: a belief in the value of work, the importance of family, the dominion of God over all things personal and political . . . The pastor was a complicated man and seemed to live across some subtle divide from *life*, certainly from *happiness*, and often from the members of his congregation, still he was an admired figure on the pulpit (already mentioned) and in the church office, the scene of so many helpful—if halting—conversations, and, as the black leader of a traditionally white church (although this, too, was changing), the object of some pride, as if his position were irrefutable evidence of their forward-thinking politics and enlightened Christianity; but no one in the church—not one worshipper out of a scant few hundred souls—could have predicted the events that began to unfold on the fine spring morning in question, when the Monday Reflection Group, such as it was, convened at the appointed time, and the Reverend Thomas Mosher was missing.

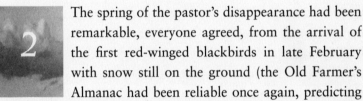

2 The spring of the pastor's disappearance had been remarkable, everyone agreed, from the arrival of the first red-winged blackbirds in late February with snow still on the ground (the Old Farmer's Almanac had been reliable once again, predicting heavy snowfall followed by an early thaw) to the return of the orange-breasted robin just a few weeks later, scouring the dormant lawns and irregular backyards still sloped, stumped, and littered with immovable stones—the landscape that so burdened the Puritans—for worms, to the skunk cabbage pushing through the sodden earth at the base of old stone walls in the deciduous woods, through the sand alongside fresh concrete foundations in the new development communities (the Walden Estates, Hawthorne Terrace, the Minuteman Apartments) fed by dripping eaves and rain gutters overfilled, to crocuses and snowdrops and daffodils in neglected flower gardens, littered with the broken ends of planting stakes and the faded plastic tabs, flattened and scattered now, identifying last year's batch of annuals, to painted trillium and trumpets in the roadside

swamps and daylilies along the winding New England roads, modest only in habitat and in the brief duration of their bloom, followed by true forget-me-nots, and on the ancient-looking tree on the church grounds, crab apple blossoms, exploding with the wild promise of inedible fruit by late summer.

Margaret Howard, matriarch of Howard Homes, the thriving real estate business she had built from the ground up, without the help of her husband, who was a burden to her, was the first member of the Reflection Group to arrive on Monday morning. In the realtor's trade she was known for her sweet maternal smile, competitive spirit, iron will, and free use of profanity. She had loaded the trunk of her bronze Cadillac with the apparatus of her gardening obsession, planning to follow up her reflections on John with an hour or two of triage in the congregation's flower beds. Artemesia Angelis, her closest ally on the Grounds Committee, and not one to reflect—or do anything else, for that matter—before eleven, would show up when she could manage. When Margaret saw the pastor's empty parking space a grateful spirit rose in her chest and she guided her floating Cadillac into this cherished spot; she had a twenty-five-pound bag of manure to worry about, after all, persistent bursitis in her right shoulder, a possibly infected gallbladder, and an internist who had warned her about the ill effects of heavy lifting. The car reminded her with the gentle ringing of an electronic bell to pull her keys from the ignition, and she did, stepping out of her chariot-on-tires with some pride of ownership. She slammed the door behind her, pressed a button on her key ring to automatically lock the car with a *chirp*, and set out across the lawn in her high heels.

The pastor was not on Margaret's mind that morning. Her son Bradley, a ne'er-do-well just like his father, had sleazed his way up to the real estate office on Saturday asking for a handout. And on his motorcycle! Bradley was a college dropout, a constant source of worry and embarrassment who somehow felt entitled to every penny she had ever earned against odds that he would never *fathom*, a devious loser who dreamed of spending her legacy on motorcycle parts and elaborate bongs. She had done the right thing, as difficult as it had been, kicking him out of the office and ordering him to Easy Ride his chopper off the property. What if a potential client had picked that moment to drive up? The nerve it took to walk into her place of business with his hair all hanging down and *probably unwashed*, dressed from head to toe in black leather—she knew what those biker getups cost—and then to smirk about it, parading in his knee-length boots past all the employees, who just loved to gossip about her family life and looked at her, after another one of Bradley's visits, with pity in their eyes, *Pity!*, for the woman who signed their paychecks every month, imagine the idea! It seemed like Bradley had spent an hour revving his engine in the parking lot before he finally peeled out into traffic. Since then, Margaret had been able to think about nothing else.

She arrived at the back door of the church in a state, stopping, for a moment, to frown at the flower beds, which would need a thorough going-over before she could even think about planting seedlings. With one hand on the railing she cleaned her heels with a tissue, cursing, under her breath, all mud, sloth, tardiness, and her ungrateful child, who might as well have been *adopted*, as little as he reminded Margaret of herself. The Reflection Group had been her brainchild fifteen years earlier, her first period of "crisis" as a parent, when Howard Homes was finally taking off and Bradley's adolescence—a Holy War that she would rather forget—had driven her to a closer study of the Scripture; participation was purely voluntary, and since the Group convened on Monday morning, the slowest day at the church (in the afterglow of Sunday, most everyone felt *prepared* to accept God's grace for another week), Margaret was often disappointed by the turnout. The pastor had disappointed her further by delegating authority over the Group to Kate Moore, the assistant minister, a humorless woman who wore men's clothing and obviously cut her own hair, and she, in turn, had given the Group over to the laity, making monthly appearances in blue jeans to cloud their reflections with lesbian propaganda, or so Margaret believed. She finished cleaning off her shoes and let herself inside the church, turning on the lights in the stairwell leading down to the Sunday School Room in the basement, which flooded at every rainstorm and smelled unpleasantly of standing water. Had she come early? The children's desks had been stacked in an orderly fashion against the wall, and Margaret could just make out the words HOLY SPIRIT on the chalkboard—erased poorly, she thought. She set up a chair for herself in the middle of the room, sat down, and opened her Study Bible to the bookmarked passage in John (13:33, "My children, I am to be with you for a little longer; then you will look for me, and, as I told the Jews, I tell you now: where I am going you cannot come") and read quietly, moving her lips without making a sound; soon she was aware of the empty room with its poor fluorescent lighting, the buckling linoleum floor, a smell of chalk which reminded her of schoolchildren, and she was stricken with her greatest fear, that she would die alone, unloved by her family and mourned by no one, and her shoulder, which had been quieted by a new prescription, gave a sudden throb as if it had been listening to her heart, a sympathetic torment to distract her from a deeper problem, so she winced in pain, closed her Bible, and stood up, wild, for a moment, with her discomfort, before her practical genius returned, sending her into the corner for another folding chair—a simple remedy, in an empty classroom, for loneliness. She opened the seat with her good arm and placed it beside her own. Then she sat back down and resumed her reading as if nothing had happened at all.

Artemesia Angelis found her working on the flower beds an hour later, draped in a denim smock and wearing aerating sandals over her Stride-Rites. Margaret had left the stinking basement short of an hour and changed into her gardening clothes. She was quite a sight, a prim and heavyset New England lady in spikes, stomping violently on the ground.

"Need any help?" Artemesia asked, watching her friend with a little awe. Her mind was still buzzing with the pastor's "sphere" sermon from the day before, and it was all she could do, beneath the windows of the parsonage, to put one leg in front of the other.

"You can carry all my junk over here," Margaret answered. "My shoulder's been acting up again, and the doctor says no lifting." She believed Artemesia to be slow on the uptake and, in religious matters, something of a heretic, but her worship of Margaret's self-confidence, obvious to everyone who saw them together, more than made up for these shortcomings. Artemesia was a loyal friend, overly generous in her opinions, and kind to everyone in the church regardless of their beliefs or social standing. Margaret directed her toward the gardening equipment and started in on a monologue. "Guess how many in the Reflection Group today? Is the suspense killing you? Solamente uno, Margaret Howard, who reflected like crazy in that *shithole* of a basement all by her lonesome. Things are really changing around here, dear, and not for the better if you ask me. And I don't have to keep my voice down because the pastor isn't even here! He could be out tomcatting in the a.m. for all we know . . ."

Artemesia had a moment of uncertainty when faced with the Cadillac's open trunk, but she rallied, and picked out Margaret's spade, her English Hand Fork, and her favorite trowel, all from the Smith & Hawken catalogue, and started back across the lawn.

"What about Kate Moore?"

"Oh, she's probably home writing love poetry," Margaret said, trying to approximate, roughly, on her circuit around the flower bed, the re-icing pattern of a Zamboni. Why couldn't Bradley have stuck with playing hockey? That's when the trouble had started: crying fits outside the rink, cutting practice after school, trading his expensive skates with that pot smoker for a skateboard, the creep, the little monster. "I can't say I care too much for this Liberation Theology, or whatever she calls it. Are you dragging my spade?"

Artemesia arrived at the flower bed and dug the spade into the ground so it would stand up on its own. "No, Margaret."

"That's stainless steel, you know."

"You're just suffering from homophobia."

"I'm not homo-anything, thank you."

"Of course not. There's nothing *ever* wrong with you."

"Well, I sell houses to them, don't I? And I don't mind saying, the gay couples really *do* seem to have a way with property. They're not afraid to sink some *capital* into an older home."

Artemesia asked her in genuine shock, "Are you wearing *stockings*?"

"I'm needed at the office later, dear."

"Margaret, you're the last of a dying breed."

She stopped aerating for long enough to catch her breath. "Did you forget that bag of cow manure?"

When Artemesia came back with the manure she complained, "Sometimes I feel like it's my lot in life to carry other people's S-H-I-T around. Do you want it here?"

"Just drop it there is fine." Margaret had finished stomping in the garden and she was sitting on her stool, unstrapping her sandals with an athlete's calm. "There's nobility in simple work. Sometimes at the office I look outside the window and see Jerry, pruning the shrubs by hand, branch by branch, or mowing the lawn on his beloved tractor, and I think to myself, *Now who has the better job?*" Jerry was her husband. After he had been "downsized" (or so he liked to claim) from a part-time sales position at the Home Depot, Margaret had hired him to keep the grounds around Howard Homes. "And I tell you one more thing, he's not out the window wishing he was in my office, answering phone calls."

"I was more complaining about the smell," Artemesia said.

"You could be the IRS," Margaret added, "now there's some dirty work." Artemesia's husband owned a lumberyard that earned him a small fortune, mostly through graft and unfair hiring practices, and his reputation in the community—the whispers, the snobbish contempt—made Margaret feel protective of Artemesia, who, it was plain to everyone, was a trusting soul. Though Margaret believed in honesty when dealing with the government, she had sympathy for Angelis's tax problems, having grown up in the fierce Yankee culture of New Hampshire, home, until recently—the crime!—to the most militant state motto in the country, LIVE FREE OR DIE. She knew something, too, about whispers and shiftless husbands. "There's an extra pair of kneepads in the trunk, or you could shovel."

Artemesia considered the spade beside her and the bag of manure on the ground, feeling overwhelmed, all of a sudden, by a sense of responsibility, and a little nauseated by the prospect of handling that stuff with a shovel, but she wanted, for Margaret, to appear strong. Her house was a mess and under permanent construction, her eight-year-old, after failing a series of tests, had just been transferred to remedial classes, and there had been talk, just the night before, of frozen bank accounts, not to mention her blood sugar following the yield of her high-risk money market account. Whatever happened to Governor Dukakis and the centerpiece of his failed presidential campaign, the Massachusetts Miracle? If only that man hadn't climbed into a *tank* to prove he had the goods to be Commander-in-Chief! If only miracles, *divine* miracles, would return to Massachusetts in the form of an infinite sphere and spread the blessing of His love from Boston to Brewster!

"Hello!"

"Sorry . . ."

"Kneepads or—"

Artemesia pulled the spade from the ground, raised it, and split the white plastic bag open with a single stroke. She would shovel cow manure for Margaret because it was lowly work, each spadeful would sicken her, and she would be *profoundly humbled*—perhaps her hands would blister—and the stinging pain would bring her closer, so much closer, to the everlasting love of God.

"You can pile it over here first," Margaret told her, setting up her stool nearby.

But she was horrified by the substance of her burden! All the richness of the earth chewed by animals bred for use or slaughter, passed through an intricate digestive system and some hopeful agricultural process to rid the cow manure of that which made it natural, leaving useful nutrients intact, of course, man's ingenuity and God's will, in a terrible combination, spilling from a plastic bag and vaguely stinking at the end of her shovel! It was all too much, simply too disturbing, and Artemesia dropped her spade, stumbled a few paces away, and sat down in the grass, about to faint.

"Take a deep breath," she reminded herself.

"Artemesia, dear," Margaret asked, "are you all right?"

"I'll feel better in a second."

"You're so pale!"

"I think I need to speak to the pastor," Artemesia said.

"Well, that might be hard right now, seeing as he's not in the parsonage. What that man does with himself in his free time I'll never know, Monday after the sermon or not . . ."

"You're wrong about him," Artemesia replied, newly serene. How could a man of such holiness be capable of adultery? And even if he was, did it really matter? Compared to all the wounded grace that fairly emanated from his heart?

Margaret went back to her gardening with the same blind dedication that had brought her to the pinnacle of the local realtor's trade, despite the naysayers and a fiercely competitive market, that had won her the respect of the Chamber of Commerce and an influential term as chairperson of the Local Redevelopment Corporation, that had intimidated her husband for thirty years and finally, through brute force, reduced him to a hopeless state, that had belittled her only son and driven him into a profound and continuous rebellion. She dug with a Hand Fork and shoveled with a spade and pulled her stool to another spot and did the same all over again. All the while, Artemesia sat behind her in the grass, looking peaceful and a little dazed. Margaret watched her every now and then with a growing anger that she would later regret. Finally she tossed her Hand Fork to the ground and asked, "Just how long do you propose to wait?"

3 Did the Reverend Thomas Mosher see a final sun-rise through the old distorted glass of his bedroom window, or was he already gone by morning? Did he wake up on his back, cold, as always, despite a great piling of covers and the space heater hum-ming by his side, casting its orange glow, and wonder in the chilly half-light, *Why am I alone?* Did the quiet of his bedroom high in the eaves of the parsonage, and the shabby bachelor's order (he stacked his books along the wall and on his desk be-side neat piles of papers and notes; he owned two identical pairs of dress shoes and lined them up each night inside the closet; he kept the throw rug, which he had never cleaned or vacuumed, in the perfect center of the room) offer little com-fort, in fact, did his circumstances fill him with a *crippling doubt* and seem to speak openly of his *estrangement from the world*? After he was gone, and the members of the church began to wrestle with his sudden disappearance, a consensus formed that the Reverend Mosher had been suffering before their very eyes, but from what affliction no one knew—they

had never thought to ask what troubled *him*, despite the sadness that had bathed him, they remembered now, like a mantle, or the fact that his smile had seemed to require so much effort, and his touch, as they filed out of the church each Sunday morning, had left them strangely cold. Thomas had fooled them with the language of faith and optimism! Was his final Sunday sermon, baffling to so many with its references to an anonymous text in Latin, *a dead language*, he kept emphasizing, an instruction manual for reading the events to come? Was he aware, as he delivered his text with a monotonous low fervor, that hardly anyone was listening? That even fewer would remember his parting words? Or was he speaking to God alone—the same God who, in His omnipotence, would recognize and understand, as they couldn't, the temptations of his boundless sorrow?

Bethany, her husband thought when he woke up alone that fateful morning, three days into his latest banishment from the marital bedroom, lying on a leaky yard-sale water bed that he had purchased to fulfill a teenage fantasy (sex, beer, and floating, as if on a dirty cloud) and had set up in the apartment over the garage, with a confusion of hoses and some gravitational difficulty, only to have his wife announce, "I will never fuck you on that thing." So the water bed had leaked away in isolation all that winter, soaking the indoor/outdoor carpeting he had installed himself (even his son had refused to help him with the job), until, with springtime surging through his veins and granting an uncanny intelligence to his scrotum, Bethany had decreed for the third time in as many years that she needed "space to think" and he was reunited with his grand unfinished project to ensure the future of their marriage, a "fornicatorium" separate from the house, no telephone, no E-mail account, no demanding kids, just the water bed, a set of Velcro straps he had bought from a high-class catalogue, and a bathroom cabinet filled with tubes of lubricating jelly. It was Bobby Caruso's special torment to sleep in his dream house of unlimited orgasm by himself.

He loved sex! and thought about it constantly, he loved the nervous moments before the act and the guiltless nuzzling afterward, the way that sex could interrupt, like nothing else, the passage of the hours, he loved the difficulty of insertion, the strange position of our sex organs on the body, he loved the *thump* and *slap* that made him think of dolphins, and the little squirting sounds, but most of all he loved having sex with Bethany, his beautiful wife, while she treated lovemaking (with him, anyway) like a necessary chore. He was faithful to Bethany even in his fantasy life, where she ruled him tenderly, usually wearing something leather, holding, more often than not, a steaming muffin tin straight from the oven (he also loved muffins) and suggesting pornographic scenarios the real Bethany would never have abided; in the rare event that they did have sex his wife kept very quiet, worried openly about the kids, heard phantom noises in the basement, and had been known to check her watch, but lately her desire for him, iffy in the first place, had all but absented itself from her body, that beautiful, unbelievable body, such a gift whenever he was allowed access, so soft, so hard, so flat, so round that even he believed she must have come directly from the hand of God.

It took some effort for Bobby Caruso to roll himself out of the water bed, stained a greasy "walnut" by the previous owner, and plant his feet on the soggy carpet. Marriage to Bethany, as he saw it, had been a verified miracle followed by a series of rude awakenings—the first came on their honeymoon in Sicily, when she had refused, despite the cost of the hotel suite, to *swallow*, not a catastrophic loss, he had decided in the end, and they had thoroughly enjoyed their remaining weeks in the ancient sun, giddy newlyweds in a foreign land, eating their weight in seafood and cannoli, slipping from their clothing at the slightest provocation (okay, so maybe Bobby had been reduced, once or twice, to masturbating guiltily beside her while she slept off a bottle of the "local" wine). Once they had returned home and established a regular pattern he calculated a significant reduction in blow jobs, but so what? He still enjoyed the rest of her body—that is, until the unexpected arrived, EARLY PREGNANCY, a spirit-breaking wallop from which he would never, ever recover. Sure, he loved his son madly, but what kind of trade was this? His sex life for a baby boy? Six years later came a daughter with terrible colic, fraying Bethany's already tender nerves and bringing to an end the last habitual intimacy of their marriage, the occasional back rub, while the latest rude awakening, he figured generously, was Bethany's rejection of his winter's masterwork, the fornicatorium. He wanted his wife more than ever, and didn't have the heart to speculate about what else, in his sexless conundrum, could go wrong.

Bobby crossed the driveway in his pajamas and bedroom slippers, disturbed by the singing of the birds, which sounded, that morning, like nature's special taunt for the separated husband. Inside, his wife would just be finished with her shower, directing the morning activities in her royal-blue terry-cloth robe, hair wet, perhaps a towel draped around her shoulders, in a foul mood that made her even sexier, to his mind; in the early days of their marriage she used to slice his muffin in half, smear it lightly with butter, and put it in the toaster oven, a selfless act, considering she was also in a rush, but he could no longer look forward to that bit of morning erotica. Now he was lucky if the children left an extra Eggo waffle for him thawing on the countertop. Bobby rang the doorbell and waited for an answer, trying not to think about how many neighbors might be watching from their windows.

"Who is it?" his six-year-old daughter, Jessica, yelled behind the door, loud enough to startle him.

"It's Daddy, cough-drop. Can you open the door?" The girl was such a tyrant that she chose her own pet names, employing them on a rotation that he could never quite figure out.

"Who's cough-drop?"

"Open the door for Daddy, please."

"Who's *cough-drop*?"

"Open the door, Jessica."

She began to laugh hysterically, cut short by her older brother, Devon, who finally opened the door for Bobby. The boy was awfully introspective for twelve and so nervous that he bit his fingernails down to stubs—although the latest development, thanks to the older kids at his school, had been his interest in rap, right down to the baggy jogging suit he was wearing now.

"Devon!" Jessica yelled, because her voice knew only one volume. "You ruined everything!"

"Morning, Dad," the boy said, heading back upstairs in his artfully untied low-tops. He told his sister, "Shut up."

Bobby dreaded reentering the family melodrama, the yelling, the tears, the constant need for discipline, the testing of his will to punish—but never without love—and during Bethany's "trial periods," when she made him sleep above the garage, his authority, with the children, was noticeably undermined. The marital bedroom, as it turned out, was the seat of all power. And his children (especially the girl) had been born with an ex-

21

pertise in manipulating power structures; at the very worst she might end up a union boss, at best a presidential biographer. (Jessica lacked the charisma, he thought, to run for President herself.) Children demanded everything you had, and in return they offered you report cards for signature. They shared nothing! On his last birthday Jessica had presented him with an atrocious drawing, which would have been fine had it been of something sweet, like a butterfly, or a ladybug, or a pretty flower, but she had given him a huge *self-portrait* in Magic Marker. Her mother had taken dictation for the caption, "Jessie takes a walk in the woods." *And gets lost*, he had thought to himself, beaming with his best version of the father's proud/touched smile. Bethany had suggested that he hang the picture in his office, so he dropped it off at the frame shop and promptly forgot about it. When the shopkeeper called the house a month later he paid dearly for the oversight! And all for the sake of this child who was shameless, greedy, inscrutable, loud, and had made it her personal project, from the time of her colic, to see that Bobby would never have sex again for the rest of his life. Jessica followed him into the kitchen with an annoying attachment, dragging her favorite handbag, a gift from Bethany's mother, who was suffering from the late stages of Alzheimer's and lived—such as her life was nowadays—in a nursing home over by the Danvers shopping mall. Bethany hadn't been to visit her since February (at least) and he had chalked up her recent mood to *guilt*, and her abiding sense that she had failed her mother.

"Mommy's upstairs," Jessie reported, "combing her lovely hair."

"Is she taking you to school today?"

"I *think* so."

"Did you sleep well?" Bobby asked because he felt like he

should, pulling a coffee mug down from the kitchen cabinet.

"Yes," she answered, sitting down at the table to resume a messy bout of cereal eating. "I got scared and slept in Mommy's bed."

"You don't say."

"I have a purse!" she yelled.

"I can see that, Jessica."

"We're out of muffins!"

Bobby poured his coffee and considered the merits of earplugs, although there might not be a substance, he figured, natural or synthetic, that could muffle the sound of his daughter's voice.

He spoke to Bethany once that morning, without incident, on his way upstairs to use the shower. She had already dressed for work in the tight-fitting beige suit she saved for springtime, and it took all of his willpower not to thank her for so thoroughly sexualizing the drabbest of all shades of color. Instead he met her at the bottom of the stairs and compared notes with her on the day to come, who needed to be where and for how long, what to have for dinner, something about a meeting running long and her car beginning to sputter, and once they had reached an agreement, on terms that confused him, they parted ways. How could she be so, well, *functional* when they hadn't slept together in six months? The bathroom was still humid with her steam and he soaked up all he could, standing in a puddle of her rinsing water; with the shower running and his eyes closed he imagined that Bethany's hands, and not a tiny fraction of the municipal water supply, were gliding over him, touching his shoulders and the middle of his back, working slowly down his chest to the lower regions of his body, warming him with sensual love. Every knucklehead in his office envied him after seeing her wedding picture on his desk, making the standard joke about wife swapping; his friends at the tennis club were forever dropping hints about mixed doubles; his little brother Sam, the dateless wonder, worshipped him for his good luck—but all the admiration in the world meant nothing if Bethany didn't want to fuck him anymore.

"Bye, Daddy!" his daughter yelled downstairs, disrupting his thoughts. If he made a recording of her "Bye, Daddy," and sold it to the military, they could use it to drive dictators underground . . .

"See ya," he called back, meant only for her mother. Just a word would have cured his morning frustration, anything at all: a curse, a snide remark, some meaningless formality; he waited for Bethany's answer while the water heater lost its muscle and his shower turned lukewarm. Bobby heard the door to the mudroom slam shut downstairs and opened his eyes to the ghastly salmon-colored bathroom, emptied, suddenly, of all sexual potential. He felt a telltale release in the area of his scrotum as his wife entered the attached garage. *Too late.* The shower went completely cold.

Bethany felt crazy when she didn't take her Zoloft, and on the morning of the pastor's disappearance she had gone thirty-six hours without dosing, a deliberate oversight: the side effects of her 200 mg-a-day prescription had been bothering her for a while now (sweaty palms, dizzy spells, nausea), and she was trying, in spite of the best medical advice, to detoxify. As a result she had lost her appetite, not that she ate regularly to begin with, misplaced her car keys until Jessie, her little savior, found them by fishing through the bowl of junk mail on the kitchen table, and forgot to wear her wristwatch, an anniversary present from Bobby—but which anniversary?—that had never seemed all that sentimentally important before *right then*, the moment when she touched her wrist in the darkness of the garage and found that it was gone. Somehow the morning's imperative propelled her forward, and she reached over a three-month pile of recycling to engage the automatic garage door opener. Jessie waited patiently in the front seat of the car, safety belt already fastened, singing "Part of Your World" from *The Little Mermaid*, the VHS tape which Bethany had used too early and perhaps too often as a mind-and-body pacifier for her daughter. Jessie's hunger for the familiar seemed to have no bottom. Ariel, the mermaid who longs to be human, had been Jessie's first obsession in life, and over the course of the last two years she had filled her room with every relic of the animated movie on the market—most she had come by honestly on holidays, the rest were a direct result of bad-faith negotiating at Toys "R" Us. Jessie's public tantrums arrived swiftly and were furious in force. Once she had wanted a replacement magic wand *so badly* that she had fallen into a trance on the aisle floor, convulsing in front of a stranger's shopping cart, a performance that had shaken her timid father and sent Bethany, once they had carried her, still twitching, across the vast parking lot and driven her home in silence, straight to her secret store of dope, a vice she had picked up, actually, from a therapist, although she rarely indulged in more than a few hits, and had stopped seeing that particular quack when he dropped to the floor at the end of an afternoon session and started sucking on her ankle. Compared to *that* little episode, Jessie's fascination with an animated mermaid seemed downright healthy. How she loved her daughter for the way she got just what she wanted, for her uncompromising will and fierce devotion to her toys! Bethany mistrusted the Disney Corporation for their treacly product that had so entranced her children, for their cynicism, greed, fake feminism, and multicultural hocus-pocus, but she had to admit, few things made her happier than listening to Jessie sing her favorite hymn from *The Little Mermaid* with its selfish-spiritual refrain about wanting more and more.

And now she couldn't risk the trip upstairs to get her wristwatch, not with Bobby mooning around the bedroom, ready, she knew, to launch into an impassioned defense of their marriage, and, when he had finished, remove his pants or open up his bathrobe in the hope that she might be feeling merciful that morning. The thought of one more conversation following this model left her heartbroken. But her wrist felt weird without her watch and she could see it on her bedside table, a place where Bobby, scanning the room for clues about her inner life, would find it and accuse her, after the family dinner (an awkward charade for the children), of being not only insensitive but ungrateful. Yes, in his case she was often both. Or had she left the anniversary watch in the bathroom? If so, the crystal would fog up, compelling Bobby to deliver his "water-resistant vs. waterproof" lecture, certain grounds for a divorce . . .

Without realizing it Bethany had climbed into the minivan, and she found herself already in the driver's seat, clutching the steering wheel. The garage door had retracted to reveal a beautiful spring morning. Jessie sat beside her, fishing through her handbag. Time ruled Bethany when she didn't take her yellow pills.

"Aren't we going to school?" Jessie asked, lifting her head from her task.

"Right," Bethany repeated, "school."

After a short time her daughter said, "Get moving!"

Bethany obeyed and jerked the car out into sunlight. She worried more about her driving when she felt unstable than she did about screwing up at work, a nowhere job in Human

Resources that Bobby had found her through "his people"—maintaining files, basically, on the thousands of jerks who worked for Bobby's company, a high-tech subsidiary of a conglomerate that made everything from refrigerators to microchips to missiles. Bethany managed her corner of the office, oversaw performance reviews, checked the odd reference when necessary, and specialized in performing exit interviews, asking questions from a script—written, it seemed, by a clueless Grand Inquisitor—and filling in the answers on a standardized response form. ("Did you feel your contributions were appreciated by your supervisor and others?" *Mostly, yes.* "Did you have the appropriate equipment and resources necessary to perform your job?" *I'd say so. That's a fair assessment.*) What finally became of this all-important survey data, who knew? The office park where she worked was just off Route 128, two exits north of the office park where Bobby's division was housed, a landscape of parking lots and bright green grass and gleaming silver office towers rising from the woods.

"Devon!" Jessie yelled when they passed her brother's bus stop around the corner, excited to see a familiar face in the outside world. But Devon ignored them, having adopted, once he reached the end of the driveway, an aggressive hangdog posture he had learned from watching music videos. His warm-up pants hung noticeably lower than they had in the kitchen a few minutes earlier, and he was wearing, despite the weather, a black knit ski cap pulled down to just above eye level.

"Why doesn't he look?" Jessie asked.

"Because he's your older brother," Bethany answered, "and he's a boy. Boys do strange things, if you haven't noticed."

"I don't like boys," she announced with great authority. "Not if they won't wave 'hello' to me."

The statement moved Bethany to wave at her daughter.

"You can't *wave*," Jessie protested, "you're taking me to school!"

"Who says I can't?"

A thoughtful look crossed Jessie's face and she asked, "Mommy, are you losing it again?"

"I don't think so," she answered, not being entirely truthful. "I'm just adjusting my medication, that's all."

"Like aspirin, you mean?"

"Yes," she explained, "like aspirin, only stronger for adults."

"What's it called?"

"Zoloft."

"*Zoloft!*" her daughter repeated, laughing maniacally.

"It is a funny name, I guess."

Jessie rolled down her window and yelled outside the car, "Zoloft!"

Bethany took a detour on the way to Jessica's Montessori School and passed the Pilgrims' Church, the spireless center-piece of "historic Old Town," *firstly* because she couldn't bear another minute without thinking of the pastor, and the church, in her mind, was so thoroughly his; *secondly* she remembered wandering in one Sunday morning looking for a consolation that would stick, and somehow she had not discovered Him, but *him*, the only man that she had ever loved unselfishly; *thirdly* wasn't happiness within their reach? Her marriage was a failure, and though she loved her children down to their little bones, Motherhood alone was not enough (she didn't have the strength for the female martyrdom routine), and the pastor was unmarried, repeat, a single man; *fourthly* she had repeated the church Covenant in good faith, but she had her doubts about this God-in-Christ business, while Thomas Mosher was a true believer and still trembled when they held each other, listened to her every word and knew her machinations better than her husband; *fifthly* their love seemed an impossibility and still it persisted, even though, from the first acknowledgment of their shared condition, they had known only the sweetest agony and lived a secret life of phone calls, long drives in the countryside and after-hours meetings in the parsonage; *sixthly* love made Bethany a minor-league stalker, and she drove by the church as often as she could.

In front of Jessie's school, watching as her daughter adjusted the strap of her oversized handbag, Bethany's eyes welled suddenly with tears and she swore to herself, and not for the first time recently, that she would go and visit her mother at the nursing home.

"Get a grip!" Jessie cried when she saw her mother's tears, jumping out of the car without asking for a goodbye kiss. Such a small girl, trying so hard to know everything—would she remember her mother as a fragile being who broke her home in two? Would she remember her childhood as *tragic*? Or maybe it was just the lack of serotonin reuptake inhibitors in Bethany's system that gave everything that morning a gauzy, After-School-Special quality.

"Who's picking you up today?"

"Ulla!" Jessie answered, already running toward her independence. "I'm not stupid!" Security was tight at the Montessori School, and Bethany waited in the idling minivan while her daughter rang the children's buzzer. Sandra, the most annoying of all her teachers, answered the door and let Jessica inside, giving a quick and unfriendly wave to Bethany. Such a harsh judge of working mothers! And this from a woman who wore baggy sleeveless dresses to flaunt her wealth of armpit hair, who owned the most expensive clogs they sold at Sonny's Shoes and lived, rumor had it, with her boyfriend in a Volkswagen camper! Those tufts of armpit hair had been Jessie's favorite topic of conversation for a solid *month*, they had even given her nightmares, and somehow Bethany was irresponsible? One day she would have to tell Sandra about the confusion she had engendered in Jessie, the Scotch-tape-and-cat-fur episode, the way she had stood up on her chair one morning at breakfast and announced, "I'm growing a beard, Mommy!"

A familiar dread visited Bethany on the highway as her minivan joined the stop-and-go traffic, and she turned on her radio, set permanently to NPR, which she found soothing, especially on her morning commute. But the news anchors annoyed her with their constant prattling on—the oh-so-smooth delivery, their faintly disapproving tone—and the emptiness of her commute, suddenly, seemed overwhelming: so many cars of so many different makes and models filling four lanes in both directions, how could she not wonder who these people were, absently picking their noses, talking sweetly into their mobile phones, sipping coffee from bulbous travel mugs that adhered, somehow, to their dashboards; every now and then she caught sight of a distinctive car or a familiar face, but most were strange to her, and while the traffic slowed before the next blind curve on snakelike 128, she catalogued her neighbors: that executive in his Mercedes with a fistful of rings, the MD applying lipstick in her mirror, that car pool full of grim white faces . . . Why this daily exodus to the Great American Workplace? To office buildings with unnatural lighting and no ventilation? She understood the problem of the mortgage payments and the credit rating, the new appliances and improved home electronics systems, and the children, of course, who needed the right "tools" for their education and clothes that would not humiliate them in the schoolyard; she understood the rudiments of the market economy and did her very best to participate, spending slightly more each year than her annual salary, hoarding her scant vacation days, and she even went the extra mile by voting in obscure primaries and midterm elections barely covered in the press, but somehow, in aggregate, *it was all so depressing*, and the fact that her family had everything they needed was not a comfort but a threat, and she felt it on the highway, trying to cross two lanes to reach her exit, and she felt it in the parking lot outside her office, gliding into her neat diagonal space, and she felt it passing by the grid of cubicles on the way to her perimeter office with its laminated "wooden" door, and only the Reverend Thomas Mosher, who cared nothing for the things that money bought, could take this empty feeling from her soul.

She called him for the first time at 10:05 and got the answering machine in the parsonage, hanging up before the beep. Anita, her secretary, had decided at nine o'clock to take another personal day, so Bethany had requested, and received two hours later, a temp to handle the phones. Her name was Pam, "from Danvers," the woman offered, a classic townie with feathered hair and a spiderweb tattoo on the fleshy part of her left hand. Bethany gave her a tour of the supply room ("You got lots of Wite-Out," Pam remarked), pointed out the bathrooms, which Pam would visit with an alarming frequency during their time together, and brought her to the vending machines—the scene, later that afternoon, of a "scene": Bethany had gone in search of a Diet Coke and happened to stumble onto Pam in front of the snack dispenser, on her knees, one arm thrust inside, trying to steal some candy.

"Any luck?" Bethany asked, standing in the doorway. Pam, if that was her real name, had gone to the trouble of taking off her burgundy leather jacket and spreading it out beneath her.

"It took my fuckin' change," she said, and smiled faintly. Bethany ended up buying her a package of Reese's Pieces, signed her time card for a full afternoon, and sent her back to the North Shore. She called the pastor again and left a message, something discreet about needing some understanding, and she spent the rest of the day rewriting a memorandum on the Family and Medical Leave Act (FMLA) that was destined only for recycling bins, the thought of which—families in distress, stray paper—made her miss the pastor all the more.

On her way home from work Bethany stopped at the parsonage and rang the doorbell. She left her car running in the driveway, the voices of "All Things Considered" leaking from her open door. When Thomas didn't answer she went back to the car and rummaged through her glove compartment for a pen, writing him a dirty, blasphemous note,

> Dear Rev. Mosher,
> I am in a dilemma. Coming to your church makes me very horny. I have tried the route of self-pleasure in the pew but found it disappointing. After the sermon this Sunday, will you fuck me?

knowing better than to sign it with a name, but he would know, he would know. She folded the note carefully and wedged it in a conspicuous place beside the door latch, pleased to feel the blood rush to her face. All the way home she thought of Thomas reading the note in the parsonage, and this imaginary congress helped her face the prospect of seeing her husband, a man who, of all things mysterious and supernatural, had come to believe in the clairvoyant powers of his groin.

Thanks to Ulla, their Swedish nanny, the Caruso household was humming perfectly that night. The table had already been set for one of Ulla's heavy meals; the dishwasher had been run and emptied; the children's laundry had been washed, folded neatly, and deposited in their respective hampers at the bottom of the staircase. How the nanny maintained such order, Bethany would never know. Three days a week Ulla spent the afternoon watching the children, and the rest of the time she was a graduate student in geology at Harvard. They had found her through their neighbors the Swensons, an honest, hardworking family who still chopped their own wood in the backyard and attended the Pilgrims' Church every Sunday—and who struggled, in a jaded time, to convince the neighborhood that the ideal surface of their family life hid nothing shady. Bethany envied Ulla's youth and effortless androgyny: she was tall and lithe, shaved her thick black hair close to her elegant head, and had the biggest blue eyes Bethany had ever seen. She wore T-shirts and ripped jeans exclusively, and didn't walk so much as glide like an insect light enough to balance on the water's surface. Jessie loved her fiercely. Her cooking, however, was another story, and Bethany's nausea returned at the dinner table when Ulla lifted the tinfoil off the baking dish and revealed to the gathered family her rendition of finnan haddie. Bobby sat at the foot of the table with a stupid cheerful grin, one hand on his after-work Samuel Adams. Thankfully Devon had retired his ski cap for the evening, and since he loved Ulla in a different way, he stared quietly at his plate, ready to blush when she addressed him. He had left the headphones for his Discman around his neck, cord dangling below the table. And Jessie, restless girl, knelt on her chair blessing everything with her magic wand. Ulla sat beside her filling the plates and sending them around. The head of the family table was a lonely place, Bethany thought, chin resting on her hands, watching Ulla charm and feed everyone.

"*Tack så mycket!*" Jessie yelled, having learned a little Swedish to impress her beloved nanny. "Everyone say *tack!*"

"*Tack*," Devon answered first, and blushed a deep, reassuring red. Bobby followed with an obsequious "*tack*" of his own, still smiling, maybe it was something in the watercooler at his office, or this beer was his eleventh—

"Say *tack*, Mommy!"

Bethany obliged her to get it over with. "Please don't take this personally, Ulla, but my appetite might not be up to finnan haddie tonight."

"Are you sick?" Ulla asked, already digging in. She ate like a horse and it never showed! Come to think of it, Bethany had never seen an overweight Swede in her life. Is it possible that being earnest burned calories?

"My stomach does feel a little shaky."

"I love it!" Jessie pronounced, cream sauce dribbling down her chin. For good measure she blessed Bethany's plate with her wand.

"It's really good, Mom," Devon added, trying to ingratiate himself with Ulla.

"I'm just warning you," Bethany told them, "at some point I might have to lie down." She stuck it out for a while, ignoring Bobby's plaintive stare from across the table, and listening to Jessie describe for her captive audience a lunchtime dispute between two of her classmates, mediated with great skill, apparently, by Sandra the judgmental hippie. Bethany ate three green beans and a new potato until, without thinking, she took a mouthful of the creamy haddock. Low tide! The dairy cow's gone fishing! Bethany excused herself and rushed upstairs to brush the rank taste of finnan haddie from her mouth, using, by default, Jessie's bubble-gum-flavored toothpaste, filled with sparkles, which only enhanced her suffering in the short run. Once again she was reminded that children's products had a way of traveling beyond their rightful boundaries, like, well, children themselves.

Now the pastor would not leave Bethany's mind, and she took to her four-poster bed from Ethan Allen and fell into a *nonplus*, worrying not about his whereabouts (not yet) but about their love and its predicament, how she, a married woman with two young children, could ever free herself to love him openly, and he, a minister of the church, could ever free himself from public opinion and accept her, never mind the different colors of their skin, still a problem in Massachusetts even though it was no longer supposed to be (in private the pastor spoke about the subject of *race* with some bitterness), and her children, innocent bystanders to it all, were quickly catching on that maybe something wasn't right between their parents, soon they would turn dark, start acting out at school and requiring sessions of Kiddie Therapy where they would scream their lungs out during role-playing exercises and beat inflatable "parental figures" silly—enough, she thought, I can't take it, and sandwiched her head between two buckwheat pillows.

Ulla stopped in before she left and gave Bethany, still lying down but no longer smothering herself, a progress report on the children. Both of them had eaten well, enjoyed their nightly TV fix—no graphic violence, one hour of PlayStation maximum—and had gone off to bed without whining too much. Their father (the beast) had already kissed them both on the forehead, and had recently retired, with briefcase, to his apartment-in-exile. Now it was time for mother's nightly blessing! Bethany apologized for escaping early from the dinner table and thanked Ulla for her patience; she tried to give the nanny some extra money for her trouble, but Ulla refused the offer quite briskly. How were graduate students, who could afford it least, capable of such altruism? Downstairs Bethany locked the front door and activated the alarm system, downed a glass of white wine in two quick gulps, turned out all the lights, and headed up to Devon's room. A few months earlier they had let Devon install a lock on his door for privacy, another wise idea of Bobby's, and since then she hadn't been able to set foot inside. Adolescence, or the behavioral part of it anyway, had started visiting the boy in preparation for the final showdown.

At the first knock Devon answered, "Yeah?"

"I came to say good night," she told him through the door.

"So say it, then."

"I just did, Devon."

"Then we're done, right?"

Bethany tried the door for the hell of it and he immediately started rustling around inside. She wondered if Bobby's pornography collection had become, between the two of them, a point of bonding. "What's going on in there?"

"Nothing, Mom," he promised.

"Sleep well, then," she answered, giving up the fight for her son, which lately had begun to seem hopeless. She worried that Devon was changing before her eyes into a suburban monster, the kind of unkempt boy who "tagged" mailboxes and set stray animals on fire with lighter fluid. Devon answered with a sullen, "Night, yo."

One down, she crossed the hallway diagonally and found Jessie in her nightgown, eyes wide in excitement, having just dumped the contents of her handbag on the floor of her room. Bethany swooped in and bundled her daughter in her arms to friendly squeals, lifting her over to the bed, where she deposited her among a petting zoo of stuffed animals, each with his or her own name, psychological profile, and genealogy. She turned off the overhead light while Jessie chattered with a group of her animals.

"I'm glad I don't have to sleep in the garage," Jessie said as her mother tucked her in.

"Well, your father's not actually *in* the garage."

"He's in the water bed!"

"That's right."

"I hope he floats away," she said, and giggled.

"Be careful what you wish for," Bethany instructed.

"I was only joking!"

She had the sweetest little yawn! Bethany felt her maternal fascination rising, mixed pleasantly with cheap white wine, and lunged to kiss the nearest part of Jessie's body, her left ear. After a short giggling session they had a conversation about where Ulla lived, and with whom, and why, the upshot being that Jessie wanted her to move in with them.

"She can sleep in the garage," Jessie suggested.

"Then where will Daddy sleep?"

"With you!" Bethany had forgotten that within the heart of every child lurks not a libertine but a family-values Republican, and she fell silent. "Mommy?"

"Yes, Jessie."

"Isn't Ariel the prettiest?"

Bethany carried another glass of wine to bed and stayed up for a while flipping channels on the television, disappointed, as usual, by her lack of options. Here a "verité" detective show, there a teenage sex soap, across the way a newsmagazine that had planted explosives in pickup trucks to make a story more dramatic, all to be followed up, later, by the accident-filled local news and garish talk show comedy. At least the wine tasted good and she was near the phone in case the pastor called, not that he would—ministering to the congregation kept him busy at all hours, and she hadn't been able to tell him, yet, about her latest trial separation from Bobby. She was angry (1) at herself for being miserable, (2) at the Networks for putting so much crap on television, (3) at Ulla for the finnan haddie debacle,

(4) at her husband because he was her favorite scapegoat when her medication wasn't working right. She was also (a) tired, (b) nauseated, and (c) depressed. Probably she was (d) premenstrual. She missed the pastor terribly, and wanted, if nothing else, just to hear his voice . . . Suddenly, with this last thought, it dawned on her that maybe, just maybe, weaning herself from the Zoloft had nothing at all to do with her volatile mood (although it couldn't help matters); it had been years, of course, since she had known anything to compare her desperation to, but wasn't she in love? With a man she couldn't spend her nights with? And wasn't love, above all else, *painful*? She turned off the television and closed her eyes, letting the images of disaster and celebrity fade from her mind, until she was alone with her desire, and his absence, a miraculous discomfort that made her feel like a saint or something, at the very least a Holy sufferer.

O *Thomas*, she thought, *where are you?*

On the morning of his final Sunday sermon the Reverend Thomas Mosher was preoccupied with a nimbostratus cloud that seemed to have formed in the sky above the church grounds, threatening a rainy Sabbath for his congregation. He kept checking the cloud's progress in the window while he wrestled with his temperamental notebook computer, some fly-by-night IBM clone that the Council, in their infinite stinginess, had purchased on the cheap from a local dealer in reconditioned office machines. First the hinge on the screen had broken, and the pastor, to keep the top of his computer upright, had been forced to stack his dictionary and thesaurus behind the thing and lean the screen against it, an arrangement that worked fine as long as he didn't need his reference books, which he often did, meaning he had to close the screen and remove the dictionary, say, from its anchor position, triggering some kind of automatic shutoff system and consigning whatever work he had just been struggling with to binary oblivion. His printer was another story, just as maddening, a donated LaserJet something-or-other that required him to hover overhead and pull each

sheet of typescript out as it rolled through the manual feeder; left to its own devices, the machine doubled as a surprisingly efficient document shredder. How many pages had he lost to its hungry innards? How many paper jams had he been loath to clear? That morning all the pastor needed was to give the text of his sermon the final once-over, and in record time—twenty minutes—he had managed to print all twelve pages of the revised version. Since he was on a roll he thought he might try and check his E-mail, but his external modem, when he plugged it in, was not responding to the usual commands. The nimbostratus cloud had been growing darker in the sky, suspending the appearance of the morning, and Thomas stepped outside to rescue his Sunday *Globe* from the rain that would surely follow. He scanned the paper over breakfast, "Mostly Sunny," the meteorologists had predicted. They were so often wrong, why didn't they just admit their ignorance? The weather was a minor passion of his, and he often tuned in to the late local newscasts to watch the Doppler radar make its clockhand sweep over all the firmament, identifying patches of precipitation, biomorphic rain shapes, and tracking their movement in the lower atmosphere. The weather's ever-changing face seemed to him an utter mystery. Even if the meteorologist, with his tailored suit and mindless patter, pretended to have it mastered—the brightly colored radar screen, after all, merely told them what was already happening, and an honest extended forecast in New England would have gone something like:

Monday:	Can't tell
Tuesday:	Who can say?
Wednesday:	Won't venture a guess
Thursday:	Out of range
Friday:	Hubris! This is Heaven's business, and not for the likes of men

He picked through the front-hall closet looking for an umbrella and came out with a vintage pair of galoshes, in ten more years they would be "antique," just one artifact, out of many, that filled the hidden corners of the parsonage, and reminded him, as if he needed it, that he was tenant in the home he lived in, the latest in a long succession, going back two hundred years, of men (and recently women) who had ministered here, and lived with their families, for half of that time, under the same patched roof, full of phantom leaks, that he did. Had the galoshes belonged to Samuel Puryear, pastor of the Pilgrims' Church for thirty years, who had stepped down from the pulpit tearfully, against his will, in 1963? Or to Harrison "Hal" Chambers, who followed him and, much to the alarm of the conservative members of the congregation, became a leader in Boston's antiwar movement?

The pastor liked to open up the church himself and let the Sunday air in first, before the energetic choirmaster, Mike Flynn, alcoholic-in-recovery and leader of the Tuesday night AA meeting, cranked up the pipe organ and led the uneven choir through their paces at nine-thirty; before the head usher, Stephen Silva, shuffled in with his undertaker's air and Dostoevskian beard (in contrast to his appearance Silva owned a family seafood restaurant, a Go Kart franchise, and a cozy bed-and-breakfast on the outer Cape) to prepare the coffee urn for the after-sermon social hour, arrange the cookie platter, and polish the pewter offertory plates with perhaps too much reverence; before Kate Moore arrived in her Toyota pickup with her dog on an extend-a-leash, coming early to coach the morning's lay reader on his or her technique; before the elder widows of the congregation either hobbled down the aisle or were wheeled by professional attendants, eager to gossip in the rear pews, to compare notes on the latest change in medication or experimental treatment, and to share with the pastor, once he came over to pay his respects, their outrage, finely calibrated, at the latest unforgivable transgression committed by a child, church member, roommate at the nursing home, or career politician. They spoke in the elegant cadences of a bygone age, and though there may have been, on the surface, much to separate the pastor from them, the elder widows, in their own oblivious way, had *accepted him* from the moment he was called to lead their church. They were women who had married young and lost their husbands, but for a few, very early; raised large families on their own to revere tradition, just to watch them all disperse to places like Irvine, California, and Seattle, Washington; they had seen the certainties of their childhood fade slowly and then disappear; fought loneliness and broken hips, cancer and emphysema, and survived it all, faith in God and family intact and *hearts wide open*. The children squirming in their seats throughout the morning prayer may have been the future of the Pilgrims' Church, but the elder widows, with a sparkle in their hooded eyes and love in their arthritic fingers, were evidence of the Congregational faith's great promise: that Christ the Mediator spreads His Fountain of Grace among the children of a living God.

No rain yet, the pastor found when he opened up the front entrance and stepped outside for a minute, and by force of wind the ominous cloud seemed, at last, to be drifting east, toward Grace Church and the conservative Episcopalians, Tories in the past and now, under the energetic rector Skip Waterbury, crusaders against Anglican Modernism, although Skip, after watching his attendance drop steadily, had recently begun coopting the methods of his ideological opponents by sponsoring Tuesday night writing workshops and inviting Christian folksingers to perform with his choir of perfectionists. And they were sore winners on the softball field—at least the Catholics had creamed them (18–2? St. Mary's third baseman coached Varsity at Holy Cross and they platooned at every position), a fate the Pilgrims' Church had avoided only by failing to reach the seven-player minimum. St. Mary's had offered their *children* (three players between the ages of six and seventeen) but the pastor had refused their "charitable donation" out of principle. Out came the beer coolers for a forfeit celebration! Perhaps the nimbostratus cloud would take a right turn after soaking Grace and pelt St. Mary's ten-foot-high statue of the Virgin.

Back inside the pastor took his customary seat in the last row of pews and granted himself a moment of reflection. He had been told all his life, first by his mother, brought up Baptist in Virginia (she had come North to attend a women's college, married young, and assimilated into New England's first religion), and then by a series of Sunday school teachers and ministers, that a church was never empty, that the Holy Spirit filled the air and underwrote the creaking planks and settling timbers. He had seen truth in the idea until, as an ordained minister himself, he started every Sunday morning with a moment just like this, and it seemed to him, after gaining some experience in the matter, that he was *perfectly, profoundly alone.* There, underneath the stained-glass windows of the Puritan saints, the pastor felt as if he were *lost in a great wilderness*, a sensation familiar to the Elder William Brewster, layman of the First Church of Plymouth, standing before the famous Rock in the highest window, flanked by Governors John Carver and William Bradford, and the Deacon Samuel Fuller; and to John Winthrop in the pane just below, arriving in Salem Harbor aboard the good ship *Arbella*; and to the minister John Harvard (lending his Grace to the balcony), who left that feeling on his early deathbed; and to Thomas Hooker, on the western wall, driving the Evil One from the Connecticut River valley; and to the good Anne Bradstreet, poised at her writing desk; and to the heretic Anne Hutchinson, tried as a Jezebel and jailed in her Eden for instigating the Antinomian Controversy. One stained-glass window stood out most of all, however, and each time, on Sunday morning, the pastor's eyes caught sight of it, he lit with a sense of the *familiar*: The window portrayed John Eliot, missionary to the Roxbury savages, standing beneath a shade tree and offering, with a look of charity, his Indian Bible to a sun-drenched Native, pictured in face paint and loincloth, who weighed the Puritan's gesture with a faint hostility. The pastor recognized himself in both halves of the picture—Eliot on his father's side, founders of the New England faith, the Native on his mother's, descended from Africans and West Indians kidnapped into slavery—and as a child of two opposing worlds, all things being equal, he could find a home in neither. But this quandary was only a beginning:

What if the historical roles had switched and he, part savage, had been elected by the children of the missionary class to lead them out of darkness, of savagery, and into the Divine and Spiritual light of the Creator? What if he had failed them? What message—above all—should he deliver to the inheritors of this spoiled Eden? Of all the variable shapes that God had taken in the minds and languages of men, was there a single understanding great enough to enclose the pastor's *soul-sickness*, to *empty him*?

> *Deus est sphaera infinita cuius centrum*
> *est ubique, circumferentia nusquam*

Or, roughly translated for the purposes of his sermon that morning, God is an infinite sphere whose center is everywhere, the circumference nowhere. He expected a disquisition on the subject to strike some members of the church as being hopeless, but Thomas no longer cared to appease his critics with spiritual sound bites and easy inspiration. Let them roll their eyes and grumble in their seats, cough throughout and punish him at the offertory plate; let them whisper behind his back at Fellowship, stuff the suggestions box with anonymous complaints, and threaten to raise issue with his leadership at the next church meeting . . .

So where was his sudden revelation? The Scripture's voice answering his loneliness with the Son's offer, *Come to me, all who are weary and whose load is heavy; I will give you rest*? Silence? Too late to constitute an answer to his prayer, the rain cloud finished passing overhead and the missionary Eliot's window filled, from top to bottom, with a gentle light, refining the colors, and the outlines, of the pastor's melancholy. He heard a sound, then—the choirmaster, whistling a pop song on his way up the steps, and calling his name from the entryway, "Thomas?"

"I'm here, Mike."

"Do you reckon we missed the rain?"

When the house alarm woke Bethany early Tuesday morning from a deep sleep she had a premonition about the pastor, that he no longer loved her, and that she would never see him again, this while she shot from her bed out of reflex and rushed to the hallway, the better part of her awareness slow to follow. "It's just me," Bobby called out over the nerve-grating alarm, and turned on a light in the front hallway. "Since when did we change the code?" By this time the children had come to their respective doors and looked out with worried faces. "It's just your father," she told them, and sent the children back to bed. For some reason, probably the "emergency situation," they took her directions obediently. Bethany had started to wake up now and her heart, tender muscle, was still pounding as she descended the stairs. Bobby squinted at the alarm's keypad in his pajamas, looking, as usual, swollen and foolish. The phone rang before they had time to disable the alarm, and Bobby went into the kitchen to apologize to the police. The security system had come with the house, a five-year-old contemporary Colonial, and over that time they had averaged a full-fledged false alarm every six months. Two more alarms in their basement, for Carbon Monoxide and Radon, cleared the house intermittently, although testing had never showed unhealthy levels of either toxin.

"This is ridiculous," Bobby complained after he had finished with the police department. Bethany had already disabled the alarm and restored an uncomfortable silence. In his hand Bobby carried the reason for their trouble, a small stack of Oreos. "Why should I have to break into *my own house* for cookies?"

"It's not the time," Bethany told him, trying to keep her voice down, "and I'm not the one who set the alarm off, am I?"

"Don't get testy with me, Beth."

She ignored his desperate use of the diminutive. "A minute ago I was fast asleep and now I'm standing in the front hallway."

"So I'm sorry."

"I can't do this right now," she told him, heading back upstairs.

"What's the alarm code anyway?"

"Jessie's birthday for the eleventh time."

"You know I'm not good with dates, Beth."

"Then comb your fucking memory . . ."

Devon seemed to have gone back to sleep already, either that or he ignored his mother's knock, but Jessie, slightly traumatized by the alarm, called out from her bedroom, "Mommy?" She wanted to sleep with Bethany again, and wouldn't take "No" for an answer. Bethany relented, carrying her down the hall, and they climbed underneath the thick comforter together. First Jessie wanted to share one pillow. Then she wanted to talk, and Bethany, trying to appease her, made the mistake of mentioning Bobby's Oreo run. From that point on, only the threat of being returned to her own bedroom would quiet the girl down. Bethany knew there was no way she would sleep that morning, not with Thomas on her mind, and she was happy to have Jessie's little furnace of a body beside her. As a baby she had smelled unaccountably like lemons, and now that she was older, Jessie's fragrance was more akin to a strawberry patch. Could it be her children's shampoo? Or was she eating so many jelly sandwiches that she *shined* the stuff? Bethany stroked her child's hair until her breathing changed, and then she watched her sleeping off another stressful day of childhood, this brave and tender girl, part of herself yet something entirely other. *She is mine,* Bethany thought, knowing full well that this was an untruth, *she is not mine* being the necessary opposite, but that was love in a nutshell, wasn't it?

In the morning she handed Jessie off to her husband (it was Bobby's turn to drive her to the Montessori School) and stumbled through her pre-work routine on a few hours' sleep, stopping, twice, to check her voice mail at work for messages from Thomas. Her premonitions had always tended to the gloomy side, and she held out hope, as always, that she might be wrong. Back when she was still a newlywed, with one year left in college, and Bobby was working ungodly hours for a sadistic systems manager at one of Boston's teaching hospitals, Bethany had always imagined the worst when he was running late and hadn't called, alone with her anxiety in their tiny rented house on a dead-end street in Needham. Her imagination had worked on a sliding scale of car trouble: at the fifteen-minute mark, a flat tire; at twenty-five, a severed fan belt (she didn't know what that entailed, really, but had liked the way it sounded); after thirty-five minutes and still no call, she became certain that Bobby had been run off the road by a semi truck; anything longer and she imagined her husband trapped in the mangled hulk of his Buick Skylark, upside down, in the process of being rescued—too late—by the "Jaws of Life." So much anxiety in the days before the car phone! Bobby, self-centered as always, had chosen to mistake her irrational panic for a young wife's devoted love. "Relax," he used to say, "you're so *high-strung*." She had hated her own tears, her heart palpitations, and her foolish need, once Bobby had arrived with his briefcase (which was usually empty!) and a lame apology, to be reassured with kisses in the front hallway. Later, when they had more money between them, keeping a box of white wine in the refrigerator at all times had done the job, and once the age of psychotropic drugs arrived, a 200 mg-a-day prescription of Zoloft. But now she was without a medicinal crutch, save her dwindling supply of dope, and if Thomas—dear Thomas—didn't call her soon, she would have to stop detoxifying.

They were tired from the night's alarm, and clumsy, and short-tempered: Dad complained about the lack of muffins in the house, Boy refused to tie his sneakers, Girl hurt her elbow somehow and whined—oh, could she whine!—and Mom abandoned them for the quiet confines of her car, where she assembled, from parts on the floor and in the glove compartment, the mobile phone that she never used, in fact *dismissed* for its intrusion into "private time," but now, seeing as this technological advance might help her betray her husband more effectively, she gave in to changing times. Four unanswered and metallic rings carried her past the Swensons' compound to the intersection of Route 102, where she paused at the Stop sign, turned right, and sped off in the direction of the parsonage.

She followed the Old Acton Road, a highway since the Colonial days and still the town's major artery, past the landscaped entrance to the Walden Estates; the struggling horse farm that had been cited by the ASPCA for neglect; the regional high school, where the administration had refused, despite an order from the state, to distribute condoms in health classes; the White Hen Pantry that had just been robbed at gunpoint; Hardy's Nursery complex, which was reputed to be owned by members of the John Birch Society; and the town's unsightly Public Works garage with its decaying plows, hulking diesel trucks, and enormous salt piles that were alleged to have fouled the local water supply. Near the first major intersection she came to a stop behind a row of commuters, all stuck at the scandalous traffic light, the subject of several Town Meetings, where, so far, their elected officials had refused to change the timing, forcing taxpayers on their way to Route 128 to wait in unreasonable lines, and effecting a grassroots campaign complete with bumper stickers ("Fix the Light"), bright red buttons, and a petition signed by over seven thousand residents, thanks to volunteers ringing doorbells all over town. Bethany had never shared their anger until that morning (why did everyone want to get to work so badly? What exactly was the rush?), on her way to the parsonage to check on Thomas. She even leaned on her horn when the Honda directly in front of her failed to run a yellow light, an outburst which earned her the hands-thrown-up gesture and a long, deep stare in the rearview mirror from a sinister pair of eyes. Where was his "Fix the Light" bumper sticker? Finally she entered Old Town and circled around the church, heart, once more, pounding, until she drifted up to the parsonage and it *stopped*—the note she had left for Thomas was still visible within the doorframe, untouched by his clumsy, trembling fingers, and his car, that misguided sedan produced and marketed for the young "career woman," was nowhere in sight. *Something had gone terribly wrong*, she was sure of it now, and she stayed there for a minute longer, dialing his phone number with a growing panic, watching the parsonage for signs of life and waiting for Thomas to *pick up the phone*, as if she could will him to be there with her eyes. Bethany felt herself tingle on the surface as she drove off again, and grow somehow lighter, unable to bear the distraction of the radio, or the plain fact that he was gone.

*Such melancholy*, thought Margaret Howard when she first set eyes on Thomas Mosher at the pulpit, an uncommon word in her no-nonsense vocabulary thick with the terms of her trade (like "assumable loans," "final value estimates," and "disclosure statements"), yet she could think of no other way to describe his figure as he faced the congregation with an uncertain smile and commenced the Call to Worship. Still, she thought, this was a fine-looking black man, with lightish skin and a neat appearance, and she tried to view him as a Christian, first, rather than as a member of the Board of Real Estate, although she couldn't help considering, at that moment, a worst-case scenario whereby the pastor, having received the Privilege of Call from the Search Committee, attracted the wrong following to their quiet town, causing the market to filter down after residential property changed hands and, in so doing, lose its value. She prided herself on her company's longstanding policy of doing business with any qualified homeowner or buyer regardless of race or ethnicity; indeed, if it

hadn't been for that complaint to the State Commission in '89, filed—without just cause—by an African-American couple from Worcester with a history of credit trouble and a sense of entitlement (they had clearly lacked the income for the town house they so coveted), Howard Homes would have had a perfect record going back over twenty years. She had even hired Mrs. Lee on a part-time basis to make the Asian clients feel more comfortable, this after training her at the company's expense! In general, however, she believed caution was the best policy when dealing with neighborhood life cycles, and viewed dramatic changes in population demographics to be the enemy of stability. The real estate business, she insisted to anyone who asked, was really very simple, and success, she preached to her employees, was just a matter of common sense—and a little creative salesmanship. *Think of yourself as a matchmaker*, she told them, *between people and properties. We have inspectors and loan officers to run background checks. You and I are in the romance business. A house is love. A house is happiness.* She had used this speech so many times now that she almost believed it, but what else could she do? "Love and happiness!" she barked at Mrs. Lee on the broker's way out to the Lexus her commissions had already bought. "Love and happiness!" she drilled into the heads of her support staff so that anyone who called Howard Homes for an appraisal would feel special. Her territory practically sold itself, boasting excellent schools (W———'s public school system consistently ranked between #4 and #11 statewide), an almost nonexistent crime rate, and a variety of well-endowed houses of worship to choose from, all just thirty minutes from the Hub, downtown Boston. As a matter of fact, Margaret had it on good authority that the widow Hartigan was finally doing some estate planning and had earmarked a bequest in the low seven figures for the Pilgrims' Church, an astonishing figure for a woman with six children and eighteen grandchildren, although, it was true, they hardly visited the poor woman.

As she rose to sing the morning's first hymn ("Alleluia! Gracious Jesus!"), Margaret looked past Artemesia, slouching as usual, to the aisle where Grace Hartigan's male nurse had parked her wheelchair for the service. She appeared to have fallen asleep already! *If I have to go,* Margaret thought, *let me go before I lose my independence. Let me go before Jerry, so I won't have to live alone.* She elbowed Artemesia, who was mumbling instead of singing, and followed the lyrics of the hymn with flawless diction, trying to set an example for the Brooks children in the pew behind. Margaret had never understood why so many regular churchgoers seemed ashamed to sing, or answer the Assurance of Pardon with confidence, or approach the Gospel reading with a sense of professionalism. Artemesia, especially, who may have been a fragile soul, but possessed an unselfconscious piety that Margaret coveted— although she never would have revealed this fact to her devoted friend, believing it might overwhelm her sense of modesty. Artemesia sang a little clearer now and even lifted her habitually fallen chin, satisfying Margaret, who once more checked on Grace Hartigan. The widow's head, elongated with age, had dropped to her chest, and Margaret could see no evidence that she was breathing.

What if she had passed away right there in the aisle, with her degenerate male nurse out smoking in the parking lot and the congregation busy sizing up this sad young minister? What if the incompetent nurse had driven off with his criminal record to stuff his face with Egg McMuffins, and the widow Hartigan, beneath her placid exterior, was *hanging on to life by a thread*? With distinguished visitors in the crowd that morning and her generous bequest awaiting final signature?

Luckily, as the hymn was ending, the old woman came to

and even joined in the "Amen," settling Margaret's spirits in her pew. The young minister closed his hymnal and, after glancing at Kate Moore, who sat behind the pulpit beaming like an idiot, turned to the congregation gathered before him. The church was packed with worshippers that Sunday, and had been unusually silent during the Meditation. Even the children, so often prone to fidgeting and whining, sat on their hands and watched him politely. "Well, he's certainly cute," Artemesia whispered in her ear, an inappropriate comment! At the Church Meeting in a week's time Margaret hoped she would take the Call more seriously, when they would have a chance to pray together, raise their voices in an orderly fashion, and decide, once and for all, whether or not they were ready to welcome the Reverend Thomas Mosher into their community. Margaret glared at Artemesia for a moment before the minister started in: "Thank you, good people, for making a stranger feel at home in your wonderful church. First, before I launch into the sermon I've prepared, I'd like to say that, from my heart, these days I have the chance to spend among you are, in the truest sense of the word, a gift . . ."

"Molly!" the Reverend Kate Moore called out the back door to her AKC-registered bitch schnauzer and closest companion in life, "MOLLY BLOOM!" The dog, recently beset by vapors, lifted its head from the ground and refused to move. Kate had named the dog at first sight, when the man at the breeding farm had pointed her out with derision as the litter's runt, and Molly, looking just a little more embryonic than the others, had opened one crusty eye and *chosen her*, Kate thought, with an ecstatic surrender reminiscent of Bloom's wife. There in the breeder's spooky barn, kneeling before the panting mother and her litter of puppies squirming in the straw, Kate had fallen in love for the first time. Relationships had always seemed outside her province (technically a virgin at the age of thirty-four, she was inexperienced beyond a few "experimental" weekends in Northampton as an undergraduate, the guest of a precocious field-hockey player from Smith), and her biological clock, as they said, seemed not to be ticking at all; children, in the specific, seemed rather unruly, and she couldn't bear them after they began to speak, when they lost whatever mute charm God had given them to enter life. If only children could learn to be more like the infant Christ! Barking, on the other hand, didn't bother her so much, and Molly, bless her little dewclaws, didn't require a special console in the pickup truck, expensive day care, or college tuition.

"Come here, Molly!"

As a puppy she had simply curled up in Kate's lap while she was driving, but that arrangement hadn't lasted long past Molly's third month, when a growth spurt hit and didn't stop until she weighed over eighty pounds, minus her unattractive tail, which Kate, after doing some research on the subject, had chosen to have surgically docked. Molly stood in the truck bed now, weather providing, although this arrangement had been a problem earlier in the spring when she began her first estrus cycle, with mongrels of all shapes and sizes howling from their yards, or, if they were illegally unchained, running along behind them while poor Molly, in protective undergarments, on a leash herself to prevent escape, kept looking over her shoulder in alarm. *Invisible fencing*, Kate had thought indecorously, *my tuchis!* Mild electrocution was no threat when compared to a willing schnauzer ambling by like a canine beauty queen at thirty miles per hour.

"Molly Bloom!"

Thankfully a prescription for chlorophyll tablets had brought an end to the embarrassment, and since then Kate had taken it upon herself to restore Molly to her former health, even if it meant sacrificing her involvement with the Monday Reflection Group for a while, giving veritable free rein to that intolerant Margaret Howard, who was an ardent supporter of Governor Weld, a loutish Republican even if he *was* pro-choice. Molly had simply not been herself and the trouble, already in its third week, seemed to be taking on the symptoms of a classic spiritual crisis. Milk-Bones were her only pleasure in life, and Kate had started buying them in bulk to get through this difficult time, offering them hourly, and for the smallest acts of obedience. In checking Molly's haunches each night she had noticed an alarming weight gain, but what else could she do?

"Come here, Molly!"

The dog finally ambled over, dragging her trolley leash along the state-of-the-art dog run, and climbed the stairs to rest her muzzle, with a look of resignation, in her owner's waiting palm. Kate unhooked her collar and let Molly inside, rewarding her with the giant Milk-Bone, which the dog brought over to her favorite spot, an egg-shaped plaid cushion from the L.L.Bean catalogue, a worthy resting place for such a sensitive animal, even if they kept hiking up the price.

Since six-thirty that morning, when she had crept downstairs in her spring slippers to let Molly out for the first time, Kate had been working on her poetry, a practice she took up intermittently and considered a sideline of her life's work: praising Jesus Christ. The demands placed on her by the congregation usually left little time for her own writing, but Thomas's sermon on the "infinite sphere"—in her estimation, a work of genius—had inspired her to bring out her verse notebook and attempt to finish her latest project, a cycle of sonnets based on the eight Beatitudes of Matthew. Kate had grown up in a religious house—Father a successful businessman and church volunteer, Mother a homemaker and Christian counselor—and she had been captivated, all through childhood, by her Bible study, especially her reading of the Gospels, which told of a Jesus so gentle and wise, and so demanding of goodness all around him, that the stories and parables often made her cry, even as an adult and ordained minister. *Foxes have their holes*, she would read with teary eyes, *and birds their nests; but the Son of Man has nowhere to lay his head.* Such a sad and thrilling lifestyle choice! Her parents had always consoled her when she became overly emotional about her Bible study as a child, and they had been very good at pointing out passages that might cheer her up (like those dirty pigs hurtling over the edge of the cliff, for one). By the age of twelve she had considered herself a girl apostle, secretly entrusted to spread the word among the powerless, the indifferent, and the openly hostile, starting at her elementary school, rife as it had been with conversion material—but her shyness, deepened by the many hours she spent alone with the Gospels, turned out to be a major obstacle: every time she had prepared herself to instruct one of her schoolmates on the various lessons contained in the Sermon on the Mount, so *good* it made her feel all funny inside, she balked at the last minute. Even Amy Hauser, a sad girl with a wandering eye (an obvious candidate for spiritual counseling), had scared her away. After failing in her own estimation to spread Christ's word effectively, Kate relinquished her girl-apostlehood and promptly fell into a dark phase (relatively speaking) when she listened to the Beach Boys and joined the girls' volleyball team. Her parents, who were getting older, worried about her soul's progress. Kate still went to church every Sunday, of course, but her failure to overcome her faults

for the sake of Jesus Christ, she reasoned, must have been unforgivable. She had accepted communion in her pew, as was the
custom in her church, with the sinking feeling that she was doing her soul irrevocable harm. So why not sin freely with the
others? Smoke reefer, cut classes, fool around with boys who
rode motorcycles? She hung around the periphery of the "in
crowd" during high school, listening to stories about the weekend parties at the reservoir, but she was hopelessly square, and
no one ever thought to invite her along. In desperation she
turned back to the Gospels and found (with Joni Mitchell playing in the background) a forgiving Christ who required mercy
and not sacrifice, who dined with sinners and tax collectors
along with his disciples, and at once she felt an enormous sense
of relief. Jesus recognized her after all! Kate grew closer to her
parents again, and together they enjoyed long talks at the dinner table about the future of Christendom, or laughed about
their eccentric neighbors, or grumbled about local politics—
memories that would sustain her when her parents' health began its steep decline. First Mother fell ill with ovarian cancer, a
terrible shock, then Father had his prostate out, and they had
spent their last years, while Kate attended Wellesley College
nearby, with either one or both of them in the hospital, so
many sutures and oxygen tubes, catheters and dressings, their
bodies wasting away and, finally, *dying* in separate semiprivate
rooms one hour apart from each other—at least she had been
able to inform them both about her plans to attend divinity
school, and they had been lucid enough to tell her, each in their
own way, that her decision made them proud. In the beginning
the loss of her parents had seemed insurmountable; a combination of prayer and dedicated study helped guide her through the
rest of college, and by the time she arrived at graduate school
she had felt less like an orphan than a child of God, the inheri-

tor of an enormous gift that she would share with everyone and never be able to exhaust. It seemed to her that Thomas, with his "infinite sphere" sermon, had spoken directly to her personal history, while, at the same time, describing the dialectic of *love* and *loss* that the life of Christ exemplified and that His teachings sought to answer when he preached in his Sermon on the Mount, *Blessed are they that mourn, for they shall be comforted.*

The telephone rang at that moment, spooking Molly, who stopped chewing on her biscuit for a moment and made an endearing "ruff" sound. Kate shushed her before she went into the study to answer the call. She had sold the big house when her parents died, and once she had settled at the Pilgrims' Church, bought this little saltbox in the country, formerly owned by an eccentric who had painted gold and silver stars on the ceiling throughout—which made her think, every time she looked up, of the beauty to be found in *finitude* and the fruits of human creativity. It was Bethany Caruso on the phone, a member of the church with lovely hair, a sullen son, and an ill-behaved daughter, and whose faith in anything Christian—save the pastor's sexuality, that is—Kate mistrusted on instinct. Just a few days before the Easter holiday, the usher Silva had confided in her (though she didn't necessarily trust him either) that, while changing the floodlight on the back side of the parsonage, he had witnessed something unnatural going on between the two.

"I'm looking for the Reverend Mosher," Bethany said, "and I can't seem to raise him at the parsonage."

"Well, I suspect that's where he is, Bethany."

"So he hasn't left town?"

As usual she had asked a presumptuous question about the pastor, and Kate thought it best to be circumspect. "Not that

I'm aware of, no. We do have a full calendar of meetings this week . . ."

"I thought there might be a UCC conference, or something."

Oh, that riled her! What did Bethany Caruso know or even care about the United Church of Christ? Such a familiar tone had unseemly connotations, created the perception, as they say, of intimate knowledge, and Kate was, if anything, protective of her church and its unmarried pastor. Groupies, she supposed, were a job hazard, and she felt an ethical responsibility to fend them off and preserve Thomas's virtue. "If there were a meeting," she said, trying to control her voice, "I would know."

"Oh, God," Bethany said after a short silence.

"Is there something wrong?" Kate asked, concerned for her well-being.

"It's just that I can't find him!"

"And you tried the parsonage?"

"No," she answered. "I mean, yes. I've placed a few calls."

"I suppose he could be visiting his mother," Kate tried, "which he does quite often. She lives in Annisquam, if I'm not mistaken."

"Yes, I think that's right."

Kate hesitated before she asked, "Is there something on your mind that I might help you with?"

"Thanks, but I don't think so."

"Anything at all?"

"I'm not sure if I feel right—"

"There's no need to explain," Kate interrupted, trying, charitably, to save Bethany from making a dishonest excuse. "When he turns up I'll just pass along your message, how's that?"

"Thank you," Bethany said, sounding relieved.

"Goodbye, then."

"I'm sorry to bother you at home," she blurted out.

"Oh," Kate said before she hung up, "please don't be."

"Right," Bethany answered, "right."

But her panic would not abate, and by the middle of the afternoon, with her calls to Thomas still unanswered, Bethany left work early, making the usual child-care excuse, and drove back from the office park to Pilgrims' Church, where the Boys' Choir, under the direction of Mike Flynn, was mumbling through a rendition of "Breathe on Me, Breath of God," a hymn so common in the liturgy that even Bethany, a half-hearted Christian, knew the words by heart. She stopped at the entrance for a moment and listened, gazing up at the Puritan saints in their usual gloomy light, touched by the children shyly singing of obedience to the divine:

> Breathe on me, Breath of God,
> Fill me with life anew,
> That I may love what thou do'st love,
> And do what thou would'st do.

As she started down the aisle a few of the boys, in street clothes, raised their heads from their songbooks and watched her, their words closer, now, to a wordless mumble, while Mike Flynn, an expressive organist to say the least, rocked along to the rhythm on his bench, throwing himself at the keyboard and then tearing himself back, conducting the choir with whatever limb happened to be free. Devon had lasted exactly two weeks in the Boys' Choir, calling the organist a "freak" and the singers "chumps." When they sang during Sunday service,

Devon shrank down in the pew and seemed embarrassed that he had ever been associated with the enterprise. Jessie, on the other hand, loved the Cherubs' Choir, and even lobbied to have her favorite Disney songs included in the songbook.

> *Breathe on me, Breath of God,*
> *Until my heart is pure,*
> *Until with thee I will one will,*
> *To do or to endure.*

The choirmaster was too entranced to notice her passing through the church, and Bethany was just as happy to avoid him; the man's good cheer never faltered, and his profound source of energy seemed, to her, a little spooky. He spoke the language of Rebirth and Recovery without a shade of irony and, in general, stood too close to people. The first time Bethany had come to Sunday Fellowship, Mike had intercepted her on the way to the refreshment table, and she had been forced to watch the Toll House cookies disappear over his shoulder, one by one, while he espoused his theory about *co-dependency* among the twelve apostles.

The church office was a depressing room off the back staircase, home to a secondhand desk, an imitation banker's lamp, ancient wooden filing cabinets, a number of uncomfortable "easy" chairs for visitors, an unreliable photocopier, a telephone (with donated fax and answering machines), and not a single human touch. Early on in her church membership Bethany had been taken aback by the modest circumstances, but then she remembered a trip she had taken to Geneva as a teenager, that strangely joyless resort town, which had included, thanks to her mother's guidebook, a visit to John Calvin's stripped cathedral, with his simple wooden chair, the throne of Total Depravity, roped off in a corner of the aisle. What a bore it had been to travel with her mother, who looked absurd in a foreign setting, and had insisted on dragging her to cultural monuments! All she had wanted to do was work on her suntan and flirt with Swiss guys (if she could find them! They seemed to spend a lot of time indoors), so she sulked along behind her mother's lead, appeased, temporarily, by an expensive wristwatch, which she then lost on a hike to see an *actual glacier* somewhere in the Alps. But the memory of Calvin's chair had come back during her course of study to join the congregation, and she recognized his spirit, she thought, in the institutional feel of the church office.

When she stepped inside, Bethany found Mrs. Safarian, the part-time secretary, and Stephen Silva, the usher, silently stuffing envelopes for a church-wide mailing. They both looked up as she crossed the threshold, Mrs. Safarian smiling in recognition, and Stephen Silva . . . well, after his wife left him in 1973, the story went, Silva had sworn never again to trust a woman. Along the way he had made an exception for Mrs. Safarian, allowing her to mother him in her natural way and scold him when he displayed his more frightening side. Together, this unlikely pair was responsible for most of the congregation's grunt work. The conventional wisdom—seldom mistaken—had the usher Silva carrying a torch for his colleague, but Mrs. Safarian's marriage, by all appearances, was a successful one, even if her husband, George, liked to grumble in public about the amount of time she devoted to the Pilgrims' Church instead of tending to him.

"Let me guess," Mrs. Safarian said, putting down her sponge for wetting the envelopes. "You're looking for Thomas."

"How'd you guess?"

"Intuition," she answered. "We've had two calls already to

complain about his Sunday sermon, and Artemesia Angelis, poor dear, just stopped by to inquire about him too."

"Has he shown his face today?" Bethany asked, trying not to sound too desperate. Her presence seemed to rankle the usher Silva. He stroked his beard for a moment as if considering the right punishment for her intrusion, then went back to stuffing envelopes with a grim efficiency.

Mrs. Safarian, on the other hand, glowed with a degree of spiritual light and enjoyment that anticipated (or so it seemed to the well-tuned members of the congregation) the joys of the heavenly world. "Well, not exactly."

"I was afraid of that."

"Usually he wanders over sometime Tuesday afternoon," Mrs. Safarian explained cheerfully, "but there are days like this one, I guess, when the Lord has other plans for him. Did you have an appointment?"

"Not officially," she admitted.

"Are you all right, Bethany? You look a little harried to me."

The usher Silva kept on peeking at Bethany's throat between envelopes. "I'm fine, really."

Mrs. Safarian moistened her sponge in a coffee mug and wiped it across the flap of an envelope. "Any message in particular?"

"Just that I stopped by?"

"Ha!" the usher Silva said out of the blue.

"You shush now," Mrs. Safarian told him.

As Bethany turned to leave, the choir was repeating the fourth and final verse of the hymn, the one about eternal life, and she wished, for the first time that afternoon, that Flynn's untalented boys would just *shut up* for a while, at least until she could put her finger on Thomas, who never sang the hymns, he admitted to her one afternoon in the country, because his ear was terrible. She missed his quiet rectitude in the bucket seat of her minivan as they escaped for a few hours, and their broken conversation while she added untold miles to her odometer, and she missed the way his resistance, refreshed by time apart, would slowly give until he fell into contemplation, and she would know, then, that they were lovers and not merely fellow congregants, because *language had deserted them*, and they were alone on a two-lane highway with their guilt and their desire, passing farm stands and self-service gas stations, circling around traffic rotaries and pulling up to rural stoplights, unable to look at each other, unable to break the silence. She missed his shyness when she found a new secluded spot and parked the family car. She missed the way his good intentions changed their nature when they sat together by the roadside.

Bethany followed the back staircase out into the churchyard, and crossed the grass with a quickening step, the sound of the organ, unaccompanied now, growing faint behind her. The windows of the parsonage were still dark, and the house itself, sagging in the middle and in need of a paint job, looked, in that characteristic New England way, as if it sheltered an unhappy family. Bethany passed underneath the branches of the apple tree, suddenly afraid of what she might find out; her pornographic note would be a test: if it had vanished from its spot beside the door latch, then Thomas, against her intuition, had come back to the church, and this period of silence had a specific meaning, was temporary, could be explained away when she finally saw him again and he accounted for his sudden absence, but if she turned the corner and found her note still waiting for him—then Thomas didn't love her anymore (how could it be true?) and his "disappearance" was merely an act of cowardice, unlike him until the very moment that he had deserted her. Partway through this formulation she began to run, brushing past the unruly hedges and emerging in the driveway, still empty, until she stopped at the foot of the entrance and looked up:

The note was gone!

Dear Thomas had come back!

He was still in love with her!

She lost her head in elation and stormed the entrance, leaning on the doorbell, pounding on the door with both her fists, calling his name to the upstairs windows . . .

But the pastor never showed himself, and soon her hope, as the doorbell went unanswered, assumed a *false and sinful aspect*. Bethany was a grown woman, after all, with a career (however hopeless), a husband (however ordinary), and the requisite two-point-three children (however confused by her marital problems)—and love, no stranger to her life, had driven her to endanger her family and *lose her composure on the parsonage steps*, in full view of the neighbors. She looked around, then, trying to make sure that no one was watching, and grabbed the door latch—inspiration! She felt the front door give, waited for a moment to make sure this portent was true, and slipped inside the parsonage.

She started her amateur search outside the pastor's private office, where she noticed first, on the windowsill behind his desk, the blinking red light of his answering machine, and counted fourteen messages* from the doorway, roughly four more than she was responsible for, and she resisted the urge to listen at first in favor of moving on to the other rooms: the kitchen with its shabby linoleum floor, cheap pine cabinets,

---

*Before the afternoon was out, Bethany would listen to the pastor's messages with her fingers crossed and then erase the tape to protect herself from suspicion. She heard the following:

"homey" wallpaper reminiscent of her childhood, although Bethany's mother, all her senses intact, never would have stood for the water stains and probably would have chucked the cast-iron skillets, blooming with rust, that hung in a depressing row above the fifties-era stove. For a moment she thought she had made a mistake and let herself into an old woman's house, but

---

"Dear Thomas . . . How many times have I asked you to change your greeting? You sound so morose, much too sad for one of God's children, but I suppose you have your reasons. It's Bethany—who else—and I'm calling because we need to talk. I'll be at the office all day. Tragically. It's Friday."

"Did I mention it's Friday? Call me."

"[silence]"

"It's Kate, Thomas. I know we shared a few words at fellowship, but I just wanted to tell you again how moved I was by your sermon this morning and how much I appreciated our little powwow about the Latin translation. Such a fascinating text for discussion! I just can't get over the image of God being an infinite sphere—I mean, the implications are endless. And such a comfort! You're a gifted man, Thomas, and I look forward to learning more about the Hermetic philosophers in the weeks to come. Bye for now."

"[in whisper] Thomas, it's Bethany. You haven't called and I'm starting . . . well, I'm starting to get a little worried. Jessie was a pill in church today and I really hope you didn't mind our leaving early, there was something in your eyes . . . I'm worried. Know that I'm thinking of you always [voice in background] fuck—not now! I'll call you when the coast is clear."

"[silence]"

"Look, Thomas, if you don't call soon I'm going to scream. Really. *I'm going to scream.* It's eleven o'clock on Monday morning, and I'm having trouble concentrating on my work, so please don't do this to me, okay? I'm trying to work some things out and . . . I'm feeling more needy than usual, and I could really use some understanding . . . That's all I have to say. Bye for now, I hope."

"Just a reminder that the Benevolence Committee will be meeting at seven-thirty tonight instead of the usual six-thirty due to the ongoing plaster work in the basement. Look forward to seeing you there!"

then she saw, on the kitchen table, the *Boston Globe* opened to the Sunday weather page, a sure sign of Thomas, yes, but also that he wasn't home. Bethany took his place at the table for a while, looking at the weather map, trying to imagine what might have been going through his mind on Sunday, the last day that she had seen him. At Fellowship they had shared a moment by the coffee urn, murmuring about the size of the crowd (why hadn't she apologized for leaving in the middle of his sermon? For losing patience with Jessie's *squirming* and her *questions* and her *greedy little hands*), and Bethany's secret knowledge of that man in the Geneva gown, on an otherwise unremarkable morning, had turned her on even more than usual. Later, when the elder widows had corralled him with their canes, wheelchairs, and walkers, Jessie had suddenly appeared, running across the grass with chocolate on her face and crumbs in her hair, asking, "Mommy, can we stay all after-

---

"You're an asshole! I can't believe you're doing this to me! Someone better be sick or dying or *maimed*, otherwise your days with me are numbered! PICK UP THE PHONE, THOMAS. CALL ME."

"Hello, Father Mosher, this is, uhh, Guy from the 'Fix the Light' petition drive? When I stopped by the other day, you told me to call you early in the week. So I am [nervous laugh]. Uhh, we could really use your help in regards to getting signatures? For the town selectmen? When you have a sec, go ahead and drop me a line at [number deleted]."

"[in tears] I'm sorry, Thomas! I'm so sorry! Can you please forgive me because now I'm worried sick . . . If you're all right, Thomas, and I'm praying that you're just, for some reason, torturing me, listen—I'm begging you, Thomas, don't leave me! Not now, Thomas! Not ever! Please, Thomas, don't leave me!"

"[silence]"

"Nothing? Oh, God—"

"[silence]"

noon?" She could be so easy, sometimes. Thomas had left early, she remembered, and now it seemed strange to her—that he would cross the lawn to the parsonage without finding her to say his usual goodbye.

"Thomas?" she called at the bottom of the stairs. "Hello? Hello, Thomas?"

Up the narrow staircase she crept to the second floor, a landing with an easy chair set by the window, a dim hallway (still no decoration) with unused bedrooms for the pastor's family, a wood-paneled alcove, and, at the end of the hallway, the master bedroom, in afternoon shadow . . . She had suspected, and now she knew, that Thomas was a saint to live in such a state of deprivation: nowhere could she find the comforts of her affluent suburbia, the carpeting that muffled footsteps and uncertainty, the ducts releasing heat or, in the summer months, air-conditioning, regulating, in a matter of minutes, mood as well as temperature house-wide, the big-screen television with channels too numerous to consider, wired to a sound system to create a "home theater," all the major consolations, in short, available to the secular humanist. Thomas lived, by the looks of it, like a graduate student, surrounded by books and papers, and Bethany felt a sense of guilt just walking in, as if she had discovered something about the pastor meant to be hidden, yet, at the same time, she was thrilled to be close to him, or at least to this reflection of his soul—that's how she thought of his bedroom as she slowly walked the circumference, such simplicity and a peculiar neat disorder, the bed unmade as if in agony, a space heater, for God's sake, who still used space heaters? Ministers of the church, apparently, which might explain the *galoshes* she had seen downstairs, once wedded to the past, she guessed, outmoded products followed suit. Bethany sat down on the edge of the bed, expecting to sink on ancient springs, but the mattress, at least, was firm; she checked the label out of curiosity, a superficial impulse (she knew) that only broke her heart when she saw the brand name "Perfect Sleeper," what an incredible idea! An outpouring of affection for Thomas sent her sprawling on the yellow bedsheet, where she grasped for his memory as if it were something she could touch, a substance like skin, a body emanating warmth and sexuality like the man himself, her lover, who had promised her once—against his will—that he wouldn't leave her, not ever. She had never been able to watch him sleep! Now all she could do was clutch his bed as if it breathed, feeling Arminian about his absence and insatiable about his *prick*, far beyond, in any secular way, missing him.

And a strange thing happened: as the minutes passed she began to feel herself in a consoling grasp, some mysterious warmth that guided her, gently, to the floor before the pastor's bed, where she knelt, elbows on the mattress, in the *prayer position*, hands clasped, eyes shut tight, mind, as it was supposed to be, swept clear. She heard a ticking in the empty room. A truck drove by the parsonage in low gear, engine whining; adolescent laughter drifted over from the churchyard, upsetting the idyll of the afternoon. The warmth had deserted her now and she opened her eyes. How much time had passed, exactly? Why hadn't she been able to pray for his return? The bedroom had undergone a change, shadows deepening, the surroundings growing less, instead of more, familiar, and she felt the chill of unwelcoming air, as if the pastor's *soul* had disappeared.

What was the source of the pastor's case of melancholy? What inner sense divided him from Christ the savior and the fellowship of other men? Was there something in his character, the members of his congregation wondered after his disappearance, that had served to distance him from the same salvation he had elucidated in his Sunday sermons, promised in so many pastoral visits, conjured during his service of the Holy Communion with the invitation *Come, Holy Spirit, come, Bless this bread, and bless this fruit of the vine. Bless all of us in our eating and drinking at this table that our eyes may be opened, and we may recognize the risen Christ in our midst?* How could they begin to read his motivation in the rituals he had performed with some clumsiness, perhaps, but always with the purpose of a true believer? What about his written profile, a document so impressive that the members of the Search Committee had overlooked their first mandate, to fill the upstairs bedrooms of the parsonage, empty for so long now, with sleeping children? How would they ever come to understand this deeply spiritual man who had, without warning, abandoned them, or begin to heal their wounded hearts with His forgiveness?

In truth they knew little about the pastor's background, just what he revealed in his ambitious sermons, filled with scholarly investigations into the traditions of their faith (his symposium on Augustine's recently discovered Dolbeau sermons was considered to have been the first disaster under his leadership, sabotaged, some believed, by members of the Council who resented paying the airfare and expenses for the guest speaker, an Augustine scholar and practicing minister from France, whose arrogance and poor language skills hadn't helped), and those personal experiences that he let slip in private consultation—most would agree that *spiritual guidance* was his real talent—in order to provide solace for the worried, peace for the ailing, and understanding for the overly self-aware and borderline despairing. The members of the church knew that his mother had encouraged Thomas to join the ministry all throughout his childhood, creating a rift with his father, an engineer, jazz buff, and practical atheist (this from a sermon about dissent among the disciples titled "All in the Family"). They also knew that his father was a man of deep political convictions, having brought Thomas, as a boy, to a number of rallies and antiwar demonstrations ("Emerson, Gandhi, and Me") and that, when he passed away from a particularly virulent form of lung cancer ("Ashes to Ashes"), Thomas and his mother had followed his instructions and organized a memorial service without speakers or a eulogy—just a quartet from the Berklee School of Music playing Coltrane's *First Meditations* suite in its entirety: "Love," "Compassion," "Joy," "Consequences," and "Serenity." They knew, of course, that his mother was black and from the South, his father had been white and from New England—and they had gleaned (and furthermore intuited from life experience) that the Moshers' decision to live together and have a child of mixed parentage had been, at the time, a matter of great controversy ("Glass Houses," a brief mention in "Epiphany Moments" and "The Jesus You Thought You Knew"). And while it made a large faction in the church uncomfortable, they knew, as much as they ever would, that racism, even in the placid and more progressive bedroom communities like W——, was still an everyday reality: early in Thomas's tenure, a young couple, also African-American, had attended the Pilgrims' Church on two successive Sundays and, feeling encouraged, had joined the congregation at Fellowship, only to be asked, during an otherwise innocent conversation with the realtor Margaret Howard, "Are you kin?" Meaning *kin* to Thomas, the entirely unrelated pastor *of her own church*, and while the couple came again the following Sunday, showing no hard feelings, and had even made an appointment with Margaret to do some house hunting in the area, word of the question spread and eventually filtered back to Thomas and had *set him off*, becoming, in local lore, the *"Are You Kin? Incident."* The pastor had made this awkward question the subject of his most controversial sermon by far ("Kinship"), examining the racial laws under the Pharaohs that had viewed all Jews as inferior—and though his delivery that morning had been far from hostile, and the tone of the sermon, in retrospect, had seemed to those in attendance to be quite conciliatory, it was said that some members of the Council—allies of Margaret Howard, who was never mentioned by name but knew full well the power of implication—never forgave the minister for using her slip-up to score a political point and imperil her reputation as a business person.

This is what the congregation knew about the Reverend Thomas Mosher's background, supplemented by the usual amount of rumor and hearsay that swirls around a public figure, aided and abetted, in Thomas's case, by his melancholy bearing, handsome visage, unmarried status, and secretive nature. What the members of church *didn't* know about their pastor would torment them in the days following his disappearance, and would lead to widespread speculation about his whereabouts, causing some (but not all) to forget the substance of his message, and to wonder aloud if they'd ever been so disappointed in a man of faith, or so indifferent—when they should, by all rights, have been in agony—about his fate in Heaven and on earth.

"Good God," Margaret Howard let out under her breath without excusing herself, waiting in the aisle with Artemesia for a chance to shake the young minister's hand and compliment him on his first sermon, the substance of which, to be honest, had not exactly dazzled her. Right after Benediction she had extracted herself from the pew and leaned down to exchange a few words with Grace Hartigan, but before the widow could answer that would-be nurse had boxed her out with an insincere "excuse me" and spirited the widow off to the head of the line. Now Margaret was growing restless and annoyed with the Brooks children, one of whom, the girl with the harelip, was whining at her mother's side, while the twin boys, both hyperactive little thugs, wrestled in the aisle right under the nose of their father, just the kind of spineless man she could not abide, not for a minute, especially with his children running around unsupervised. Artemesia, dressed, as usual, in her Sunday sackcloth, seemed lost in religious ecstasy, staring up at Anne Hutchinson's window with that heretic's look in her eye.

"Are you aware of how she died?" Margaret asked, ready, at the same time, to cuff the Brooks twins and their father for disobedience and negligence, respectively, on such an important Sunday.

Artemesia had spent the morning trying desperately not to look up at her favorite saint in stained glass, the charismatic and headstrong merchant's wife who had nearly brought down the Massachusetts Bay Colony with her heresy trial, dressed, in the window, in a simple gown and clasping her personal Bible to her heart. The Sunday before, during Kate Moore's heartfelt "activist" sermon about the importance of recycling, Artemesia had been visited by the sensation that she was being watched, and immediately checked over her right shoulder expecting to catch the elder Swenson boy, Bernie, staring at her again, only to be confronted by the Puritan martyr, animated in her windowpane, gazing down on her with a beatific smile. Of course Artemesia knew how Anne Hutchinson had died!

"Indian massacre," she whispered, bowing her head out of respect for the dead, "at Hell's Gate. There was only one survivor."

"What on earth is going on at the front of the line?" Margaret asked, craning her neck to get a look at the Reverend Mosher. "Some of us have errands to run."

"I'm going to the supermarket," Artemesia said, leaving an open invitation for Margaret to come along. The Super Stop & Shop was a source of anxiety for her, beginning with the parking lot, acres wide and long, a chaotic mess of shopping carts and sport utility vehicles where she often lost track of her station wagon, while inside was no picnic either, a hangar-sized maze of looming shelves complete with a separate pharmacy, video store, and mini–Pizza Hut. Artemesia always wound up at the meat counter, gazing at the family packs of cube steaks and chicken thighs despite the uneasy feeling in her stomach, the butchered meat all rosy under plastic and arranged to please the eye.

"Oh, no, dear, Jerry does all the shopping now. I'm afraid he's out of his element in the supermarket, though. The man is always forgetting something."

"Aren't those boys getting handsome," Artemesia remarked, referring to the Brooks twins, currently engaged in a shoving match. Artemesia's oldest son was only twelve and already he could grow a mustache just like his father. From the beginning he had been a little man, all muscle and bravado, destroyer of everything complicated, fragile, or unwilling . . .

"God forgive me," Margaret said, "but right now I'd pay a pretty penny for their matching scalps."

"You don't mean that!"

Her friend's shock chastened Margaret. "No, I guess not. I let my temper get the best of me."

"Because I think they're darling."

"And so do I," Margaret said, trying, once again, to be more Christian about the whole thing. Already the usher Silva had calmed the boys down by hissing at them through his dentures. "I'm just not sure how I feel about wrestling matches in the Lord's house."

Up close Margaret thought the minister was a little short, perhaps, just over five foot nine, certainly a handsome man and not *too black*, she noticed. In her opinion his coloring seemed just about right, and his eyes, behind somewhat sleepy lids, had an intelligent sparkle to them, a quality that Margaret had always found attractive. Say what you would about Jerry, as a young man he had been all spunk, the kind of man who could flirt openly with a married woman and charm her husband at the same time. Margaret introduced herself to the Reverend Mosher again and thanked him for the inspiring words, making sure to check the condition of his fingernails, by far the best indicator, she believed, of a man's character. Years of building business relationships had taught her a secret or two about human nature, and the ways we have of unintentionally revealing ourselves to others. The Reverend Mosher's fingernails looked fine, though his handshake, on the limp side, needed work if he wanted to inspire confidence in his leadership abilities. She saw no reason for the minister to be single at, what, thirty-one? Even if his last pastorate had been in nowheresville Rhode Island, couldn't he have found a good woman in the congregation? Without a wife at his side and a family in the works, this minister was going to be a real *liability*, and Margaret questioned the wisdom of the Council in calling him to Pilgrims' Church, still reeling from the Reverend Chambers's unexpected retirement in May and move to some kind of New Age retreat in Scottsdale, Arizona—though she had been relieved when

Kate Moore, in a surprising act of *realism*, had asked to have her name removed from the Search Committee's short list.

"I hope you're enjoying your stay," Margaret told the Reverend Mosher, meanwhile angling for the door. Artemesia's timid nature had kept them at the end of the line and she was not one to waste her life standing around.

"Very much," the Reverend Mosher answered, "thank you. You have quite a congregation here."

"Artemesia, go ahead and introduce yourself."

"If you'd given me the chance," Artemesia began.

"I'll be right outside," Margaret let her know. "Wonderful to see you again, Reverend Mosher."

"And you, Mrs. Harpswell."

"The name is *Howard*," she corrected him.

"Forgive me, Mrs. Howard."

"Yes, of course." She reminded Artemesia over her shoulder, "Be quick, now."

Oh, my, Artemesia thought, feeling Godly vibrations in the company of the young minister, *this is the one! He's come from a distance to rescue us!* The church had grown quiet by then, the rest of the congregation, and its invited guests, having retreated to the lawn for Fellowship. Artemesia trembled in his company. The sunlight in the doorway, at that moment, seemed bright enough to burn through her dress and reveal her soul to the eyes of the world.

"Are you happy in Rhode Island?" she asked, having summoned the courage to speak.

"It's a good church," the minister said, "with extraordinary people. We're a few miles outside of Pawtucket. Have you been there?"

"Never," she answered, still aware of the burning light.

"I find it peaceful. The ocean is a short drive away."

"But are you happy?" she boldly asked.

The minister hesitated for a moment before he answered, "It's a depressed area. *He is the joy of the upright of heart.*"

How she fell for him at that moment! Tired of the assistant pastor with her well-meaning certainties, her love of all creatures great and small, her prayers for the woods and sermons about using the right recycling buckets, green for newspaper and magazines, blue for glass and most forms of plastic . . . Thomas Mosher had *hesitated* before he spoke to her, and in this hesitation Artemesia had sensed a great pain in his heart, the essence, she felt, of the religious experience—hadn't the Puritan Thomas Shepard of Cambridge, whose writings she had studied at the local public library when she sought to join the Pilgrims' Church, counseled his parishioners to "doubt thyself much"? Her husband doubted *nothing* about himself, that much was clear: he wore far too much cologne, applied an aerosol fixative to his hairstyle until it had the strength of a helmet, forbade talking at the dinner table so he could eat "in peace," didn't know a thing about foreplay, spent a fortune on a game for which he was ill suited—golf—and set his pager on "vibrate" because he claimed it was good for his prostate. Artemesia's trembling had quieted by now, and in the interim she had become planted to her spot, waiting for the minister's direction, her face, she hoped, showing no evidence of her inward smile.

"What a morning," he said, nodding toward the sunlight. Was that a bead of sweat running down his cheek? Had the vibrations they were obviously sharing become too much for him?

"Yes, it's lovely."

A blessed silence passed between them; Artemesia imagined her patron saint Anne Hutchinson shifting in her Colonial dress and approving of their union with a simple nod.

"I should play some politics outside," the minister told her candidly. Such an honest face! And freckles too! "Care to join me?"

"Oh, I'm afraid not. On Sundays after church . . . well, it's not that exciting, really." Oh, the shameful timidity! "I usually do the weekly food shopping for my family."

"Why don't I follow you out, then," he said, and ushered her, before she realized what was happening, through the gaping doorway and into daylight. She descended the wheelchair ramp out of reflex, an indirect route, perhaps, but while crossing over its pressure-treated frame (donated by her husband's lumberyard) she intoned a prayer for the handicapped and for the elderly, a little rushed that morning, with the soon-to-be pastor—how she hoped!—following close on her heels. Margaret had been waiting by her Cadillac all that time and motioned to her wildly across the parking lot. At the bottom of the ramp Artemesia stopped and said goodbye to their visitor.

"I hope you'll stay with us," she said, bracing herself for the inevitable, a piercing whistle that Margaret produced by blowing through her fingers and reserved for Artemesia and her useless husband, Jerry. The usher Silva had set up the refreshment table on the lawn and a much larger crowd than usual was milling around, the children having shed the outer layers of their Sunday best to ruin their appetites with cookies and play a nonconfrontational variant of tag. Artemesia's sons attended church only on holidays, and even then they usually went to the Orthodox service with their grandmother, who secreted them off to her apartment afterward to fill their stomachs with Keftedes and their impressionable ears with bile.

"And so do I."

The whistle! So sharp the young minister winced in pain and the congregation, busy renewing acquaintanceships and catching up on family news, fell quiet. A dog in the neighborhood started barking in response, and Artemesia heard some-one say, "I wish she wouldn't do that." Was it Lucia Wagner, Margaret's sworn enemy on the Grounds Committee? Or Sadie Maxwell, the leather merchant, who refused to mark down her handbags after the Christmas holiday? Artemesia took her leave and suffered the humiliation of hurrying over to Margaret in front of everyone. It was a great sin, she believed, to be so full of pride as to concern herself with the opinions of the con-gregation, and she felt perfectly easy as she crossed the parking lot to Margaret's Cadillac, in full submission to the will of God.

The members of the Pilgrims' Church had welcomed Bethany Caruso from the beginning, but she often wondered, during the months of her initiation, if they fully practiced their Redeemer's love; in fact, the congregation's less admirable qualities had convinced her that, without her attraction to the Reverend Thomas Mosher, or, to be more accurate, their *mutual fascination*, she would have given up on her religious Awakening in its early stages and returned to life as a satisfied—albeit medicated—agnostic. Bethany's parents had baptized her in the Episcopal Church, and they had taken great pains to drag her and her three surly brothers to worship every Sunday. They were a ragged, disorganized family that must have been mortifying to behold in full flower: Jonathan, the eldest, suffered from a sleep addiction and dozed off like clockwork when their rector launched into his sermon; Nate, the "difficult" second child, refused to kneel when ritual called for it, and spoke openly of dousing the Everlasting Flame with Holy Water; quiet Lewis, tormented by hard-ons, hadn't been able to accept communion once his hormones started firing; and Bethany, the youngest child—a midlife "mistake"—had been forced to sit between her parents for protection, and spent most of her time each Sunday morning deflecting dirty looks and fugitive pinches from her flesh and blood. Bethany's parents had divorced when she was twelve, blaming the pressures of family life and the rector of their church for his inadequate counseling, and in the difficult aftermath, both her parents, wounded by the swiftness and finality of their breakup, had sworn off organized religion of any kind. None of the children complained—Bethany and her brothers found a bitter freedom in having single parents, shuttling back and forth between the Newton house, which their mother kept in the settlement, and their father's apartment in Brookline, using one set of rules to gain concessions from the other, manipulating the strained relationship between their parents for revenge and profit. As a teenager Bethany had been polite, studious, and wild, leading a reckless life on weekends that included boyfriends from second-tier local colleges (Babson, BU, Tufts) and drinking games with Southern Comfort, the delinquent's liquor of choice at her high school, Newton South. An unattributed pregnancy—and quickie abortion—straightened her out in time for college, where, during her junior year, she met the reliable Bobby Caruso and settled down, but why? This she could never quite figure out, not then, when her friends had tried to talk her out of getting married before she received her degree, and not fifteen years later, when she found herself with two children, a troubled marriage, a job she couldn't bear but needed for the paycheck, and the sinking feeling that something essential was missing from her life, an unnamed product that no department store carried on its shelves, and no credit card, however large the spending limit, could buy.

Enter God, or at least the first New England meetinghouse she saw when she drove through Old Town, kids strapped in back, on the errand runs that filled her weekends with despair. Sleepovers, birthday parties, movie rentals, trips to the drive-thru cleaners, grocery shopping—she was forever dropping things off and picking other things up with her car running, losing one child for the night just to gain four others who were not her own, exchanging vast sums of money for disposable goods and lamenting the passage of time . . . Would she ever experience the fabled state of Peace & Quiet? A moment to reflect on her place in the world and—dare she consider it—the meaning of life? She had tried a program of meditation and beginner's Yoga at the local Women's Center and *it sucked!* Just be honest, she thought, and call it Hippie Aerobics, that way no one would be disappointed when they failed to find nirvana in their Danskins, contorted on a smelly mat beside a stranger in a strip mall. *Exhale into a spinal twist. Good, now gently turn around.* The chanting Yoga instructor with her little pigtails and perfect posture had so annoyed Bethany that she found herself slowing down when she passed the Pilgrims' Church, checking the time and subject of the Sunday sermon, posted each week on a wooden sign that faced the road.

She skipped "Summer Impressions, Part I" (10:30) because it sounded too "arty," and "Summer Impressions, Part II" (10:30) because she was out of town. Finally "A Love Supreme" (seasonal time change, 11:00) brought her to the doorway of Christendom on a rainy September morning. Bethany peered inside and let her eyes adjust to the gloom. She had come early to escape the house, and there were a number of empty pews to choose from. The few parishioners already there talked quietly while the organist worked his way through a dramatic instrumental that shook the walls. Bethany settled into a seat near the back, looking up at the stained-glass windows and recognizing the Puritan dress, but none of the grim-looking subjects. Now she knew that Carlo and Lucia Wagner had come down the aisle holding hands, as always, and taken a pew near the front; first the husband, then the wife, had turned back and caught her eye, murmuring something between them, sharing a look, it seemed, of pleasant surprise. The Swensons had arrived next and Bethany shrank a little in her seat, hoping that they wouldn't notice her right away—she had forgotten that her neighbors worshipped at the Congregational church, and she wanted to be anonymous that morning, a stranger in the house of God.

The Swensons had recently finished building a sauna in their backyard, and just the day before Bobby had brought a pair of binoculars up from his "workshop" so Devon could spy on them. "Nudity!" Devon had cried, leading Bobby to put down the newspaper, usually grafted to his hands all weekend, and join him at the kitchen window.

"That's sick," Bobby had said, "they've got the whole family in there together, even little Pele—"

"*Dad*," Devon had whined, jumping up and down with excitement, "it's *my turn* now."

The Swensons had dressed neatly for worship and didn't recognize Bethany until the church had filled to half capacity and the service was about to begin. The children waved at her in unison across the aisle; Piotr, an ageless sixty-five, fond of big straw hats and a corncob pipe, had given her a neighborly thumbs-up sign. She waved back reluctantly and lowered her gaze. And to think that Thomas had so underwhelmed her on that first morning! She had been surprised, at first, to find a black minister preaching in Old Town, and she had followed his direction as best she could, repeating her part of the Call to

Worship printed in the morning's program, mumbling her way through the unfamiliar hymns, answering, from her seat, the Assurance of Pardon, all the while watching the minister for signs of personality, the special bearing or creative spark that separated the talented clergy from the dull; he must have something special, she thought, to be leading a congregation at his age (which she figured to be thirty) and at this time, when complacency and conservatism had overtaken the politics of Massachusetts, once considered, by outsiders, a People's Republic.

But his sermon had been a snooze! Mixing recollections of his childhood with a meditation on a Psalm about the wicked, how they scoffed at their adversaries and boasted about their accomplishments, thinking that God had gone into hiding—an important point, Bethany thought, but hardly *revolutionary*, and Thomas's delivery that morning had been inept: he stumbled through the language as if in darkness, tripping over his words, losing his place on the page so that his ideas were often punctuated by an awkward silence. Ten minutes into the sermon the pews began to creak, yet the minister preached on without improvement, turning back to the nature of the Psalmist, and on, meanwhile Bethany's thoughts had turned to Bobby, or at least a version of him that she enjoyed thinking of, the tender young husband, who had insisted, one memorable night, on *going down on her* even though she had claimed she didn't like it—how could she have known?—because it seemed, well, *sloppy*, and made her feel uncomfortable; afterward, when an unprecedented orgasm had rocked her world, Bethany held his grinning face in her hands and loved him, she remembered clearly now, *loved him so much* that her feelings had overwhelmed the present tense and opened a window into their future together, when his hair, already thinning, would follow the stencil of male-pattern baldness, his cheeks would swell with pasta and prosperity, and thick black hair would sprout from places that she wouldn't want to think about—yet she had believed, then, that his transformation into middle age wouldn't bother her, not when he could bring her such a feeling of release, make such a home for her in that confusing place, her own body . . . Thomas had fixed her attention again with his conclusion, quoting Ezekiel 37:5, "Behold, I will cause breath to enter into you, and you shall live," comparing this living breath to the spirit that moved through John Coltrane (hence the sermon's title) and then, with a look of great sadness, he had stepped down from the pulpit and joined the rest of the congregation, standing now, for the singing of the closing hymn, led by the choir, which had been languishing on the balcony throughout. Bethany's bones ached from a mixture of boredom and lust, and she felt a twinge of guilt for not knowing the lyrics, when so many around her, even the children, sang clearly, if without conviction, along with the Pilgrims' Chorus.

After the service ended, an ad hoc welcoming committee, chaired by Piotr Swenson, greeted her in the aisle, and her neighbor enfolded her in his arms, purring something about seeing the light at last. She had wanted to protest, explain to him that she had come as a mere experiment and couldn't imagine a Faith or a Community that she would join—her family and job were quite enough, thank you, she had no room for God, who, come to think of it, *was* hiding pretty effectively from the world and its problems, but she had kept her mouth shut, stepping back from Piotr's embrace and greeting his wife, also named Ulla, who kissed her on the cheek, and the children, who shook her hand politely, beginning with the oldest, Bernie, with his buzz cut, and homely Elka with her hand-knit cardigan, and handsome little Pele in a pint-sized suit and tie. Others had greeted her too, although she couldn't remember them now, and it seemed as if she had been carried down the aisle by their goodwill, although someone (Lucia Wagner?) made an apologetic comment about the pastor "finding himself," and intimated that he was better skilled at offering private counsel. It bothered her that Thomas remembered the moment they met in the entryway so vividly, when she recalled almost nothing: just that it had started raining again, and she had left her car at the far end of the church parking lot, having thought the downpour to be over, and the pastor, attractive or not, had been an obstacle on her way out. "I fell in love with you *at once*," he told her much later, after the affair had been consummated in their minds, first, and then with their bodies, and their lives, once so separate, were inevitably bound. Bethany thought it strange that, while Thomas had been choosing her to dwell in his heart, and risk his standing in the pastorate, her mind had been on the weather, and it would be months before she suspected anything of the kind.

"Why are you here?"

The question had taken Bethany by surprise, and haunted her after her first interview with the pastor, arranged with great difficulty in the weeks that followed her visit to the Pilgrims' Congregational Church. She didn't know exactly what had driven her to show up for that particular Sunday sermon, other than her vague sense that something *was not right*, and she didn't know why she had called the church office twice, leaving messages on the answering machine (Thomas hadn't answered the first time), finally getting a callback at work late one afternoon, her department in the midst of a minor crisis. Because of space problems they had packed some older files and shipped them off-site, but now her supervisor needed them for an internal audit, and the storage company had no record of the transaction, or so they claimed. The caper of the missing personnel files! As if she didn't have enough useless paperwork in her life already. She had been on hold with the surly storage people when Anita buzzed her on the intercom and said, "There's a priest or something on the line."

"Can I call him back?" Bethany asked, and returned to Office Retention's twenty-four-hour hot line, currently piping in Rush Limbaugh for the benefit of its neglected callers, something she found shocking. Did they want people to hang up, or what? Anita buzzed her a minute later, and she was happy to leave the pathetic meanderings of Limbaugh's tiny mind.

"He says now is the best time for a conversation," Anita delivered with a deep sense of weariness, as if she lost a piece of herself each time she answered a call. Bethany asked her to deal with the retentive people at Retention and picked up the pastor's line herself.

"*Why are you here?*" Thomas asked in the church office, looking squarely over her right shoulder, the stairwell outside ringing with footsteps and, from the floor below, the cheerful preamble to a Debtors Anonymous meeting, one of the many services that the congregation offered to the community. Thomas sat across from her in a patterned sweater he would later call his "Bill Cosby" after its warm and fuzzy nature and prohibitive price. Bethany had been beyond the reach of subliminal messages, however, and she stammered for a moment before she answered his question.

"I'm curious," she said. "That's why I'm here."

This seemed to satisfy the pastor, who leaned back in his desk chair and continued to study the wall behind her. She turned halfway around to see what the excitement was, found nothing, and faced the pastor again. *Say something!* she wanted to cry out, but managed, out of courtesy, to keep her mouth shut. She had experience dealing with deliberate "slow talkers" at work—in fact, her company specialized in hiring men with this fatal flaw, and just one, with the attending drawl and taste for pregnant pauses, could hold her hostage for what seemed like hours at a time. But this was not Thomas's problem: his trouble with "A Love Supreme" had been the result of a temporary slump, and that very Sunday he would give a flawless sermon about truth in politics or the lack thereof (with Bethany in audience), and his uneasiness that evening, with the last of the Debtors filing in downstairs and taking full advantage of the free coffee, was not about stupidity, or a lack of professionalism, but *overwhelming love*—

"Well, that makes two of us," the pastor said, "curiosity between strangers being, ummm, sort of pronounced."

"And how are you curious, exactly?"

"You came to our church," Thomas answered, "and then you called to set up a meeting with me, so there must be something on your mind." He finally looked at her straight-on. "Am I on the right track so far?"

"So far," she said, "yes."

"I know why you're here," he announced, charming her, despite the presumption, with the hint of a smile.

"This should be good," she answered with some sarcasm.

"May I go on?"

"Why not," she told him.

"You're here," he continued, "because God willed it to be that way. An Infinite Wisdom brought you here, and that, as far as I'm concerned, is the simple part." Bethany had expected something along these lines, and she kept quiet while the pastor finished, looking past *his* shoulder now and out the window as the sunlight drained from Old Town. Soon the leaves on the stately row of maple trees behind the church would turn and fall, and the crew from Homeless Helpers, hired on a trial basis, would rake them into piles and set them aflame with lighter fluid, trying to roast marshmallows, a misguided effort that brought complaints from the neighbors and a visit from the police department; when the Helpers saw the flashing blue lights they scattered, leaving behind the sticky remnants of their ritual, and so many cigarette butts that the volunteer members of the Grounds Committee would still be picking them out of the grass the following summer. "The hardest part is yet to come. You might decide to hear another sermon, or sit in on a Bible class, or bring your family [here the wounded tone in the pastor's voice had attracted her attention away from the twilight] to the Autumn Fest for homemade apple pie. But will you come back?" The longing in his eyes! She had imagined a more confident pitch for her soul, including, perhaps, the subtle mention of some Hellfire, or whatever innuendo passed for Eternal Damnation in the age of Wellness, but this was something else entirely.

"I'm curious," he wound up, "about what I can do to make the Pilgrims' Church more user-friendly, without sacrificing the depth of our Covenant. *Bethany, I want you to stay with us.*"

After the interview she virtually stumbled out of the church office, carrying her briefcase down the aisle while the pastor followed her, pointing out the pipe organ, which had some historical significance, and the stained-glass windows, darkened now; the world outside seemed to have fallen quiet, and Bethany couldn't wait to get back outside to her car, and away from this unexpectedly intimate encounter with a man of the cloth.

"God be with you," Thomas called after her as she descended the wheelchair ramp, lit by a single spotlight.

"*Thanks,*" she said, a response that would seem lame to her when she thought about it on Route 102, stuck in late commuter traffic, waiting for the interminable light to change. What was she supposed to say? *And also with you?* The pastor had thrown her off with his disarmingly honest opening question, and from that moment on her mind had been swimming . . .

At home that night she avoided questions about where she'd been and instead gave Bobby a hard time about bringing home pizza (again), even though the pediatrician thought Jessie might be lactose-intolerant. The three of them had already eaten and made a perfunctory attempt at cleaning up the kitchen, leaving Bethany a single crooked slice of pizza in the box. Bobby and Devon were playing Nintendo Golf in the living room, while Jessie had gone upstairs to play with her stuffed animals. Bethany had carried the box of Chardonnay from the refrigerator to the table, siphoning off enough to fill a water glass. The pizza slice they had left her was missing half of its pepperoni and she considered it for a while, letting the wine sedate her first, before she forced this slab of "food" into her stomach. The longer she watched her pathetic dinner sitting in its box, the more remote her appetite felt, and Jessie, all sweetness and bodily function, saved her from having to eat by calling from the top of the stairs. "I need help in the toilet, someone!"

"Not me," Devon scoffed, lying on his belly, just like his father, eyes tuned to the enormous Trinitron. Bethany lectured them endlessly about giving equal time to Jessie, who couldn't survive without watching her Disney tapes at least once every forty-eight hours, but they never listened. Every game of Nintendo seemed to carry the weight of their entire lives.

"Should I go, hon?" Bobby asked from the other room, an offer that struck Bethany as unusually generous.

"That would be nice," she told him, closing her eyes. The

kitchen had started rotating pleasantly and she wanted to experience Chardonnay's sweet merry-go-round in darkness.

"But, Dad," Devon whined, "this is match play."

"Help me," Jessie whimpered.

"Can it wait until I finish the hole?" Bobby asked, undoing whatever good he might have done in making the offer.

"Just forget it," Bethany said, opening her eyes and standing up so quickly that she became light-headed. She grabbed the chair for balance and called upstairs to Jessie, "Mommy's coming in a second!"

"You're a peach," Bobby told her.

"Asshole," she countered under her breath.

"Hey," she heard Devon say, "nice putt."

At her weaker moments, when Bethany felt that she existed under a black cloud, that her unhappiness at work and selfishness as a wife and mother had somehow poisoned her house, she tried to remind herself of the sacrifices she had made for the sake of her family, and the areas of mothering for which she had shown unusual patience and an obvious talent. This much was true: she loved both of her children equally. Devon had been an easy baby to get along with, sleeping through the night and smiling through his waking hours almost from day one, while Jessie, to put it bluntly, had been a horror: sickly, fussy, loud, spiteful, sleepless, and inconsolable through it all. During her "terrible twos," however, something inside Jessie had softened and she became a thoughtful and affectionate child, fond of storybooks and belly kisses, bubble baths and family trips to the Museum of Science. Devon, at that age, had turned destructive and unexpectedly sour, shouting "No!" whenever he was spoken to, and bonding only with his Tonka trucks, which he would cuddle and speak to as if they were human, then toss from the top of his bunk bed or kick all the way across the backyard. Watching her children grow had opened Bethany's eyes to the varieties of human behavior, and the endless act of creativity that is childhood.

And if she had accomplished one step of their education without flaw, sent her children into the world with a single skill that would set them apart from their peers at school, it was toilet training. Simply put, Bethany was a genius with the family potty. She had discovered her talent quite by accident when Devon, at twenty months, began to show an interest in the nondescript potty seat she had installed in his room a few months earlier, hoping to bring an end to her diapering duties. On, off, wipe, on, off, wipe—it was an unending cycle, and Bobby had been an incompetent helper. From Devon's first, tentative moments with the potty seat she had followed Dr. Spock's directions carefully, letting him familiarize himself with the equipment fully clothed, and gradually introducing him to the idea that he might want to take his pants off and climb aboard whenever he heard nature's whistle call. Devon had shown periods of resistance, whining and sputtering away from self-sufficiency (just like a man!), but she had done the right thing by waiting patiently until instinct took over again and he ascended the potty without her help—and then she had showered him with grown-up compliments. My God, what a little dupe! Mother had crushed him, and within the year he was flushing happily all by himself. Jessie, too, had been a pliant student; at two years she was already familiar with the wiping mantra "front to back," and she even had a vague idea as to why ("Girls only!" she would shout). Jessie had taken special pleasure in graduating from diapers to training pants, and in the rare event of an "accident"—which Bethany took in stride—she had quietly rededicated herself to Mother's goal, that her children should lead independent digestive lives.

The experience of so many smears and stains protected Bethany as she climbed the stairs that night, unaware of what disaster she might find behind the bathroom door. In the end the emergency was minor: Jessie had been scared, more than anything else, by the way her intestines reacted to the pizza, and she had made it to the open toilet seat as soon as nature struck—and hard. Mommy's little girl didn't smell like strawberries anymore! Still she would have to be cleaned up, and Bethany instructed her to strip and stand in one place for as long as she could manage. Jessie always seemed much happier when her clothes were off (just like her father), and while Bethany, on her knees, disinfected her sensitive skin with Baby Wipes, she lifted her arms over her head and sang the chorus from Disney's "Under the Sea" in a fake-calypso voice, trying to mimic Sebastian the lobster. Anything by Disney so overexcited Jessie that soon she was running in place and squealing, and Bethany had been forced to give up.

"Thanks!" she yelled as she ran nude from the bathroom, leaving Bethany with a pile of slightly foul laundry. Bobby chose that moment to come upstairs and "contribute" to the running of the house, hovering outside the bathroom door with his usual cowardice. Anything scatological, as a rule, sent him into the garage, where he kept his *Penthouse* collection in a storage tub, or down into the basement workshop, where, she knew as a fact, he drank beer and ate Pringles on the couch.

"Can I help?" he asked, afraid to show himself.

She surprised him with Jessie's laundry, dropping it in his arms and directing him to the hamper in the mudroom. His expression told the tale of a middle manager required, all of a sudden, to do something unpleasant *himself*, and the power of speech deserted him. Bobby turned and headed back downstairs in full retreat. *It serves you right*, she thought, considering he spent the bulk of his time "managing" other people and organizing hypothetical "projects" which usually came to nothing. The company was forever sending him away for two weeks at a time on short notice, leaving her with the same job and even more work to do around the house. And judging by her workload they were forever hiring more just like him, ineffectual white men with résumés that cried out HELPLESS WITHOUT SECRETARY AND/OR WIFE, FORMERLY MOTHER while Bethany and her mostly minority colleagues in Human Resources made their lives easy, spelling out retirement plans far superior to their own in plain English, filing forms directly with Payroll, who were unbelievably rude, computing vacation days to their fullest advantage, none of which these cookie-cutter husbands with their Strip-O-Grams and Sky Pagers deserved. Okay, perhaps she was exaggerating this last part, but Bobby's face when confronted with his daughter's *shit-smeared laundry* filled her with contempt, and, more important, revealed the depth of his willed indifference to the small realities of life.

And imagine, Bobby had had the nerve in bed that night to reach across her back and pinch her nipple! She had stayed up late after seeing the children to bed and scrubbed the kitchen, then made her rounds through the downstairs picking up debris and turning off the plain blue television screen, the very essence, she reflected, of suburban life. She balled up the empty Doritos bag nearby, and, out of spite, threw away her husband's beloved "chip-clip" too—just looking at this hopeless "invention" made her heart sink even lower, reminding her of all the stale men eating crispy snacks that would only clog their arteries and further slow their reaction time. She could see Bobby already, searching through the kitchen drawers and cabinets, yelling because he thought she was in the other room, "Have you seen the chip-clip, honey?"

And this snack-obsessed *moron* had just pinched her nipple!

She had climbed into bed long after Bobby, hoping that she had lost him to his recurring erotic dream about the flat-chested lifeguard on *Baywatch* (she had forced it out of him during a session of couples counseling), but as soon as the lights had gone out and she was breathing faintly and evenly with sleep almost in sight . . . the *pinch*! What an act of utter carelessness, leaving Bethany no other choice but to give him a sharp, enlightening elbow in the side.

"Hey," he said, "what gives?"

"I was almost asleep," she told him.

"That hurt, you know."

"And my nipple is a *sex button*?"

"Christ," he said, rolling away.

"Just go to sleep, Bobby."

"Okay," he answered, "jeez."

She blamed Bobby and his unrealistic sex drive for forcing her into playing the role of "frigid wife," because she was not, by any honest definition, frigid. Her sexuality may have become, after fifteen years of marriage and two children, a wizened animal, but Jesus it was *full of life*, and subjected her, on a regular basis, to random aches, throbs, flashes, and bouts of "the itch," never mind the generalized longing that often swelled like a string section inside the theater of her heart. A few months earlier she had carried on a near-affair with Allen Weinglass, a Title VII specialist and the only decent-looking man in her department, initiated (and by him, she reminded herself) with an exchange of flirtatious E-mail messages that had made her blush even as she knew their banter was desperately unoriginal; they had consumed each message just to delete it by mutual agreement, trying to reduce the evidence, which might have brought them trouble (who knew what power was transcribing their binary conversation? The risk, she had to admit, was fairly exhilarating), and soon they were arranging awkward encounters in the kitchenette ("Just you and me," Allen would remark, standing uneasily in the doorway, his jacket shed, sleeves rolled up to his elbows, while Bethany, also jacketless, would cross her arms and lean against the dishwasher, hoping he would stay, hoping he would go away), until the near-affair took on a life of its own, and escalated beyond E-mail and innuendo to a date for cocktails at the Parker House downtown, with a room upstairs awaiting their decision to *close the deal*, as Bobby liked to say. Bethany had breezed into the lobby that night feeling, if anything, disgusted by the symmetry of the thing, and bothered by this room that Allen had booked so eagerly, without her consent; and Allen had proved himself to be a snake, rising from his high-backed chair to greet her with an affected wink, a standard compliment, and a kiss too heavy on the saliva—at that very moment it had ended, with a hotel room, a wink, and a sloppy kiss, because having an affair with Allen Weinglass, she realized, was madness: she would have been forced to quit her job rather than face him every day, and, all reason aside, though she had wanted him seriously for a while, she loathed him, yes, that was it, she *loathed Allen Weinglass*, and the attraction of an affair had worn off long before their scheduled meeting at the Parker House, which she abruptly ended in the middle of her first glass of wine, leaving him alone with his single malt and his workplace fantasy unrealized. "Hey, what's this?" Allen asked in protest, bolting up from his chair and knocking over their candle. "Bethany, what's this?" The jilted almost-lover of a mostly faithful wife causes a minor scene in the bar of a faded luxury hotel that was slated to be demolished! "Follow me," she called over her shoulder, "and regret it." The bartender had really chuckled over that one. *Life can be so cruel*, she thought, walking through the revolving door and out to Boylston Street, topcoat in her arms and her mistake regrouping in the bar, finishing his scotch and sweeping up the honey-roasted nuts he had spilled all over the table, wondering, she thought, where his seduction technique had failed him. Bethany had absolved herself from guilt by the time she reached the end of the block, and walked in a sort of daze until she found her minivan; but a stranger in downtown Boston, acting as an agent, she decided, of divine retribution, had smashed the window on her driver's side into a thousand tiny pieces, stealing the manufacturer-installed tape deck, the first-generation mobile phone that she had inherited from Bobby, her hateful briefcase (after dumping out the paperwork—foiled!), and, she would realize later, when it suddenly became vitally important to Devon's well-being, a half-inflated soccer ball. Why couldn't they have relieved her of the paperwork too? She had lied to Bobby that night and told him the break-in had taken place outside the mall, and as for Allen Weinglass, a few months later he had received a job offer in North Carolina and handed in his notice, informing Bethany in a brisk E-mail and adding that he had spoken to her supervisor and requested that his exit interview be performed by someone else.

Truth be told, Bethany didn't think of the pastor much in the days following their first interview. Work and Family quickly reasserted their dominance over God, and on Sunday morning Bethany had awakened without the intention of going back to church, and felt, instead, an old familiar tenderness for Bobby, lying on his back with his mouth wide open, not snoring so much as *inflating* and *deflating* with the sound of a balloon. Overnight he had mostly extracted himself from his pajamas, and from the peaceful way he slept, she guessed that he was languishing, at that moment, with his favorite lifeguard. A cursory search with her right hand turned up his morning hard-on and she figured, *Why the hell not?* For once she would let her husband meet the day in the throes of orgasm, and within a minute or so Bobby was wide awake (though still supine) and thanking her in a whisper, cupping her head in both his hands and making all kinds of obscene promises . . .

"Mommy!" Jessie yelled, having thrown the bedroom door open, watching as her parents quickly rearranged themselves beneath the covers. "I want pancakes!"

"The way it works, Jessie," Bobby told her, doing a remarkable job of controlling his anger, "is you *knock* first, and then, if we're feeling up to it, we invite you to come inside." He buttoned his pajama top with some reluctance. "Is that clear?"

She frowned at him.

"Are you listening to me?" he asked again, playing the stern disciplinarian for once.

"Yes," Jessie answered, still frowning, and turned to Bethany for support. "Can you make pancakes, Mommy?"

"Just be patient," she said, already exasperated by the morning's events. The suggestion of pancake batter had sent her desire crawling back into its underground system of tunnels. *Please*, she thought, *no one say* bacon. "Your mom's a little slow on Sundays, remember?"

"Pancakes!" her daughter yelled, running off in her Dr. Denton's and leaving Bethany in the unenviable position of having to face, for the second time that morning, her husband's involuntary hard-on. A tentative daylight shined through the underlayers of their custom window treatments, and while Bobby fumed and rustled in the insulated silence of the master bedroom, waiting for Jessie to reach the bottom of the staircase, Bethany prepared herself for the next request. Who knows shame and guilt so intimately, she wondered, as the dutiful suburban wife?

"Well?" her husband asked.

"I don't know, Bobby."

"C'mon, Beth, I was *so close*," he lied.

"Look, if the moment's gone—"

"Don't say that!"

"I'm sorry," she said, climbing out of bed and heading for the bathroom, "but the thought of making pancakes for everybody sort of turns me off."

"So make muffins," he suggested.

"*That* I won't respond to."

"Oh, Beth, c'mon—"

She closed the bathroom door behind her, letting out a well-earned *Christ*, and headed straight for the medicine cabinet and her Zoloft.

Halfway through the breakfast preparations, with Jessie running in demented circles around the kitchen table, Devon transfixed by professional wrestling in the TV room, and Bobby moping around the house without offering to help, Bethany was overcome with the desire to *get out* and gathered her family in the kitchen to respectfully inform them that (1) if they wanted pancakes they would have to finish making them without her, because (2) she was leaving the house for a few hours to visit a Congregational church, that's right, go by herself to a *house of worship* in order to spend an hour or so contemplating the spiritual side of life, which, she suggested, the rest of them could stand to think about more often, instead of depending so heavily on Mother for everything from grilled-cheese sandwiches (Bobby, Devon) to reassuring hugs (Devon, Jessie) to the bedtime stories that would carry them off to sleep at night (Jessie), and (3) if they had any questions or comments about her morning respite from the family, she would answer them in due time. Only Bobby looked distressed by her announcement, asking, in his most helpless voice, if she knew where he could find the griddle, while Devon had shrugged and cut out of her speech early, worried about the outcome of a wrestling match. Sweet Jessie, in her Mermaid pj's, had merely asked, "Can I come with you next time?" showing a restraint that Bethany admired as she climbed the stairs to get dressed for church, and deepening her sense of guilt—this time for going ballistic on her entire family, especially the children, who, at eleven and four, respectively, couldn't exactly be held accountable for ignoring their spiritual lives. What had she been thinking? Well, she realized, at least I'll have something to confess this time . . . After rushing through her morning cleansing rituals (skipping the makeup round) Bethany had come downstairs to find Bobby flipping the long-awaited pancakes, and trying, without much success, to normalize the situation. Jessie sat at the table squeezing a bottle of syrup over her short stack.

"How are the pancakes?" Bobby asked loud enough for Devon to hear him in the TV room.

"Mine are gooey in the middle!" Jessie offered.

"Well, I'm sorry about that. And you, Devon?"

"They're kind of pathetic, Dad."

"Dad makes gooey pancakes!"

"Just pile it on, kids."

"YUCK!"

"WHATTUP! You're POISONING us!"

Bethany was the last to arrive at the Pilgrims' Church that morning, slipping into the same pew she had chosen the Sunday before while the pastor called the congregation to worship, and bid them to rise for the opening hymn. She flipped through the hymnal trying to find the right song, but the children's choir, seated in the balcony, had already started the first verse, and she mouthed the words as best she could, looking over the shoulder of the man in front of her for the right hymn number, coming up with #122 ("God Is My Shepherd"), which seemed to be missing from her songbook. She gave up during the second verse and instead watched the pastor, who, in turn, was admiring the organist for his appearance of joy, and she was moved by the sound of these imperfect voices—some angelic, others earth-toned, one warbling out of control—joined together for the sake of a greater song; moved by the pastor's visible pride in his organist, who had *reformed* himself in the image of Christ (she would later learn that Mike Flynn, in his darkest days, had lost his legal practice after playing fast and loose with his clients' money, a fate he blamed on the devil alcohol and the "enabling" superstitions of Catholicism); moved by the worshippers all gathered in their customary pews to praise their Shepherd, undeterred by the fact that their church was more than half empty; moved by an autumn light streaming through the stained-glass windows, a welcome sight at the end of such a trying morning; and as the hymn came to an end, Bethany felt a spirit rise within her heart—could it be true?—and spread delight where there was once frustration, filling her body with a desire that she had never known before, the longing for a

> *dwelling place*

as the choir promised, where

> *my shepherd blesses, cares, and leads through*
> *all eternity.*

The organist lifted his hands Liberace-style from the final chords, and Thomas, on perfect cue, smiled gravely from his place beside the pulpit, nodding his thanks as the children's choir, also on cue, returned to their seats in the balcony. The congregation followed suit with a collective sigh and *creak*, including Bethany, who wondered if she hadn't just experienced some kind of vision, and flushed with the possibility that God, remotest Father of all things, had made a visit to the Pilgrims' Church and noticed her, even if she wasn't singing.

A blessing!

A moment of grace and piety!

But the feeling was not meant to last, and during the pastoral prayer, with her head lowered and her eyes closed in apparent obedience, Bethany's thoughts turned back to her meeting with the pastor, how the intimacy of the encounter had surprised her, and the longing in his eyes had driven her, in a state of panic, back to her car with its four-speaker stereo and reassuring privacy—back to her children, who needed her, and her husband, who worshipped her, and their architect-designed contemporary Colonial—everything that Bethany had ever wanted in life attained (and legally) by the age of thirty-five, *yet it was all a lie*, or so it seemed to her, and she wanted—no, needed—to escape from her dull "career" and her troubled marriage, even as she coveted their security.

Why the panic, then?

Because she was afraid. Because she was . . . unhappy.

What was she afraid of?

The pastor. She barely knew him, and as a rule she didn't trust the clergy, the same way she mistrusted therapists, and contractors, and politicians—anyone, in short, who engaged in glorified fix-it work. Unlike the rest, who repaired the known, members of the clergy tinkered with the *soul*, something, as she understood it, that might not even exist! But there was something about Thomas that appealed to her, perhaps the novelty of finding a black minister in this, the whitest of communities, or his looks, which, she had to admit, caused a certain flutter below and left of her sternum, or his ring finger, that emblematic digit, hairless and sleek, unbound by gold or platinum . . .

What heresy had just crossed her mind? And with her head bowed in the act of prayer? This latest realization, in comparison to the one that followed, was nothing:

Soon the pastor wound up his morning prayer, asking for, and receiving, the congregation's soft *amen*. The familiar answer had rolled off Bethany's tongue as if she meant it. With a look of grave sincerity (she peeked) he directed them to begin the silent prayer, which Bethany had been craving since the "pancakes episode" in her kitchen, so she obliged, and in the morning stillness, with her eyes shut tight, she continued to reflect on her unquiet meeting with the pastor and his evident desire (or so she thought) to save her soul, his certainty that she had come to the Pilgrims' Church under the direction of his God, and not by her own volition. How predictable! A man who knew nothing about her belief system had casually informed her that she was living under God's control! Such *utter bullshit*, she thought, letting this profanity ring out in the silence of her imagination, hoping it would spread to the congregants in the other pews, perhaps, even, to the Swensons across the aisle, who would confront her after the service with their fingers pointed, *It was you! You put those dirty thoughts in our pious heads!* There, having raged against Divinity, she felt a little better, and waited for the pastor to break the silence with the recitation of the Lord's Prayer, the only part of the service that she still remembered from childhood.

And waited.

And kept on waiting, but the silence continued on, long past anything she had experienced as a young Episcopalian, and she opened her eyes out of impatience to find the pastor still behind the pulpit with his head bowed, and the congregation, well used to these extended moments, making prayerful use of the time. One of the elder widows snored lightly in the aisle, while her nearest contemporary (Lili Baldwin, a former pediatric nurse and fund-raiser for the Communist Party, who would herself pass away in less than a month) tugged at her sleeve in alarm. The pastor seemed to have lost himself in thought, and Bethany left the elder widows to their morning drama, watching Thomas instead, this awkward young minister in his Geneva gown, standing before his congregation wordless, alone, and in full command of a silence that grew deeper with each passing moment, and more significant, until it seemed to both reflect and answer a great collective anguish, the unspoken substance binding a group of souls into a congregation . . . The pulpit where he stood, she thought, might have been miles away, yet his melancholy (so alarming when they met) seemed to welcome her, and accept her inmost thoughts for what they were, and shelter her desire for a happiness beyond the present tense, even if, in the future, she would tempt him—and here she speculated—to violate your odd Commandment and break the church covenant to engage in sins of the flesh, because his private sorrow was that *real*, as they say, and that *intense*, and *she wanted to fuck the pastor, that was it—she wanted to fuck the pastor in her husband's bed.*

"Why are you here?" Thomas had asked unfairly to open their first conversation, and in church that morning, while the pastor gave a sermon on the ubiquity of political spin, Bethany thought of the perfect answer: *Because you will fall in love with me.* Of this she was strangely certain, and in her pew in the rear middle of the church she began to plot the unforgivable, a seduction that would—after months of the pastor's sometimes baffling Sunday sermons, the mind-numbing "Alpha" course in Christian Education, a staggering number of interminable church socials, and, most important, an *increasingly intimate* series of pastoral visits—escalate into an all-out love affair. The congregation itself proved to be a mixed bag, but she was surprised by how easily she returned to the ritual of churchgoing: rising early on Sunday morning, making sure the children dressed in time, ferrying them to Old Town with the same sense of purpose that her parents had needed to ferry her and her three brothers, cranky with a lack of sleep, to the Gothic splendor of St. Anne's in Newton. Bobby would have no part of her renewal, believing that any involvement with the church would further undermine her sexuality. Wrong again! Though the pastor was often called to visit one of Boston's many teaching hospitals, tending to the sick, or busy offering spiritual counsel to a couple in the congregation, or mediating a dispute on some volunteer committee; and though the members of the church (save the Swensons, who were, as always, loyal and generous) could be judgmental, especially the younger parents, who implied, without breaking their Christian smiles, that it was a *sin* for Devon and Jessie to have arrived in Sunday school so ignorant of the Bible; and though Thomas had seemed reluctant, at first, to spend time with her alone, pawning her off on Kate Moore, the assistant minister, who oversaw the Adult Christian Education program, or Sandy Margolis, who taught the children patiently in Sunday school—Bethany's attraction had persisted, and she finally managed to secure the pastor's undivided attention for a second meeting, at the same time of night, nearly a month after she had fled his office in alarm. The darkness outside was heavier now, and instead of Debtors Anonymous, an exercise class in the basement (taught by her greatest rival for his affections, Alessandra Palacios y Rio) provided the background din. Bethany arrived early and, finding the church office empty, took a seat to ease the pounding of her heart, which tended to race before she saw him. *All right!* Alessandra encouraged her fitness class, yelling over Abba's "Dancing Queen." *Keep it up, now! One! Two! Three!* It was Alessandra's intention to bring spinning classes to the Pilgrims' Church, and she had pledged to match any gift of one thousand dollars or more toward the purchase of six state-of-the-art machines. The pastor had come in without making a sound and closed the door behind him, startling Bethany, and she grabbed her briefcase and stood up, realizing how absurd she must have looked only when he motioned for her to sit down again. Bethany was unaccustomed to feeling flustered in the company of men—she usually brought out *their* nervous tics—and she hoped she wasn't blushing too obviously.

"Sorry about the music," Thomas said, taking a WGBH coffee mug from a rack on the wall and filling it with hot spring water from the dispensing tank behind his desk. Carefully he dipped a tea bag inside and then took his seat. He had replaced his "Bill Cosby" sweater with a button-down cardigan that she would nickname "The Priest" before she peeled it off his body in the parsonage the following spring. "Despite our limited resources," he went on, "we try to offer a wide range of church activities, some beyond the usual forms of outreach."

"Like spinning class?" she asked, trying to start things off on a flirtatious note, and slightly hurt that Thomas hadn't thought to offer her some tea.

"For a church to live," he offered as an explanation, "it needs to adapt. The world is different now than it was in 1658, or whenever the Assembly at Savoy founded our Way in England. Today we have to compete with the global marketplace, home entertainment, the media, and a creeping—" A look of concern crossed Thomas's face and he interrupted himself to extract the tea bag from his mug. Bethany watched him search for a place to throw it out; finding none, he dropped it on the windowsill behind him, a curious solution, she thought.

"Forgive me, but I forgot to offer you . . ."

"That's all right," she told him.

"Please, let me . . ."

"I'm fine, really," she answered, touched by his courtesy. "Please go on."

"Where was I again?"

"Something was creeping?" she prompted him.

"I'm afraid that's not ringing any bells."

"Spinning class!" she remembered.

"Ah, yes," Thomas said, sipping from his tea, "the Aerobics Outreach program. Not exactly my best area. Blessed are the bookish and the lame, for they end up in the ministry. Or something along those lines." Through the door Bethany could hear Alessandra's class begin to clap along to the music, a pathetic sound—there must have been five of them, and even so, their sense of timing was screwy. Thomas heard them too, and gave her what she took to be an apologetic smile. "They'll be finished soon enough."

"Oh, I don't mind."

"Good," Thomas said, leaning back in his desk chair, which gave a suggestive squeak (here Bethany's heart began to race again). "Why don't we talk about you."

But Thomas didn't mean this in the way that she had hoped! The minister, as it turned out, was only interested in her spiritual life that night, and he proceeded to grill her on the progress of her Adult Christian Education, placing special emphasis on *The Congregational Way of Life*, a dreary paperback that

Kate Moore had pressed upon her a few weeks earlier detailing the history of the church and its foundational polity. Bethany had tried reading it before bed each night, pen in hand, approaching her assignment with some sincerity, but Bobby made his disapproval quite clear, and lobbied, instead, for his beloved *nookie*; when that approach failed she had tried reading *The Congregational Way of Life* aloud to the children, but Devon, two minutes into a brief history of the Protestant Reformation, had pronounced the book "a yawn" and returned to his seat by the television, while Jessie, usually a rapt audience, kept on interrupting her to ask, "Aren't there any animals in this story?" So Bethany had given up, and later made the mistake of asking Kate, during the next education class (she arrived twenty minutes late and apologized profusely), if they had a version of the book on tape so she could listen to it during her commute—oh, the patronizing look! From a woman who had no children of her own and seemed uncomfortable around *youth*, and who couldn't possibly be aware of the demands placed on her time and sanity. And now the pastor, who claimed to be so interested in her case, had started quizzing her on *The Congregational Way of Life* as if she were a high school student, asking if she understood the implications of Christ's sovereignty, or the meaning of a "gathered church," or the importance of prayer and unanimity in the church meeting—and though he meant well, she was certain, and asked his questions with obvious care, Thomas's mini-lectures on each subject (the Priesthood of All Believers, the Meaning of the Eucharist, etc.) were more than a little patronizing. If Alessandra Palacios y Rio hadn't interrupted them, glowing with sweat and dressed in some kind of Lycra body stocking, Bethany would have been forced to make up an excuse to flee.

"Pardon me," Alessandra said, clinging to the open door.

"I'm always forgetting to knock first. What a *great workout* we just had downstairs!" Though she spoke with the accent of a European émigré, Alessandra was actually from Framingham, and had returned to Boston from the West Coast after the failure of her third marriage. She had grown used to her position as the congregation's siren, and treated Bethany with some wariness. "How are you, Bethany?"

"At the moment I'm confused," she answered, with perhaps more candor than was necessary, "but this too shall pass, right?"

"It always does," Alessandra told her with an artificial warmth, still catching her breath from the aerobics. "The question is, when will our parson here join my body-sculpting class?"

Thomas stared modestly into his cup of tea. "Well, I'm not sure about that. Probably never."

"And why not?" Alessandra asked with a pout.

"My athletic career began and ended in the ninth grade," Thomas told them, "when the basketball coach, I forget his exact name, ordered me to try out for junior varsity. He found me in the library reading—and I'll always remember this—Walker Percy's novel *The Moviegoer*, my favorite book at the time, the scene where Percy writes *to be neither pagan nor Christian but this: oh this is a sickness*. Chilling words. Anyway, I warned the coach that I was useless at sports, but he didn't believe me."

"How dreadful!" Alessandra gasped.

"I showed up to the tryout in dress socks and penny loafers," Thomas continued, the lofty tone of a sermon creeping into his voice, "which my competition found amusing. But I saw an opportunity to teach the coach something, mainly that *this* black kid couldn't even dribble with his good hand. After the first layup drill they asked me to leave. I was," he admitted, "the original geek."

"That's an outrage!" Alessandra leaned one arm against the doorway for balance while she stretched her hamstring. Her age was something of a mystery to the congregation (Bethany guessed that Alessandra was in her early fifties) and there was no denying that she had a wonderful body. "You could have *injured* yourself! Such savagery!"

Bethany felt her interview was taking on a surreal quality and she listened quietly while Alessandra settled her business with the pastor and left with an insincere apology for interrupting their meeting. Bethany checked her watch and marveled, as she often did, that time should move so swiftly.

A few months into their affair, during a weekend drive that had carried them, mostly in silence, far away from the pulpit where Thomas warned against the temptations of selfishness and apathy, Bethany would remind him of their second interview, and confess that she had left the church office that evening convinced that, due to her poor working knowledge of *The Congregational Way of Life*, she had fallen far in his esteem—as well as suspecting that Alessandra Palacios y Rio would body-sculpt her way into the pastor's affections, provided that she hadn't done so already. It was springtime, one full calendar year before the pastor disappeared, and Bethany had pulled her minivan to a stop beside a muddy field in some nameless central Massachusetts town, slightly west of Route 495. Thomas was suffering from a cold that day, and had taken Bethany's advice and spread a woolen blanket over his lap. "Do you mind?" Bethany had asked, and lit a joint that she had rolled the night before while sitting in the minivan, her family snug indoors and unaware that Mom was busy in the driveway separating *seed* from *bud* on a road map of New York State. Thomas (of all people) never judged her, and this, she thought, was an unbearably attractive quality; he was a minister, after all, and therefore had a public role to play, a script to read, a chorus to reflect on his performance—and an official "modest" costume to wear on Sundays and holidays. Sometimes, watching him deliver a sermon from her favorite pew, or listening to him chat with a parishioner during Fellowship, Bethany forgot that, when they were alone together, Thomas could ignore his sanctioned lines and *become someone else*, not a hedonist, exactly, and hardly Mr. Carefree; in her company, at least, Thomas was a man first and not a minister, and left his scriptural analysis aside to sit with her while she smoked a joint beside a cornfield; or, when she demanded it, massage the areas on her neck where the tension in her life gathered itself up in knots; or, quite frankly, reach down the front of her unzipped jeans and *bring her off* with his index finger and a well-placed thumb, complaining only if she bit his shoulder particularly hard, and never when she wept about her marriage and wallowed in self-pity . . . So she smoked half of a joint that weekend afternoon, turning her back to Thomas and asking him to perform the usual massage, which he did, listening to her theories about Alessandra, himself, and the erotic possibilities of body-sculpting . . . And then Thomas answered with his own confession that his failure to speak with her openly that night, and only about her reaction to *The Congregational Way of Life*, had been a source of disappointment. He admitted, afterward, to dialing her home number from the parsonage on three successive nights, and hanging up as soon as Devon answered (she chided Thomas for harassing her children). What was this boy, an answering service? Would they ever put the child to sleep? Finally he gathered his courage for one last attempt, when, after two long rings, Bethany had picked up herself with a weary *Hello?*

Silence. Thomas had stayed on the line for an extra moment, hoping that he would find the courage to speak.

Hello?

More of the same.

Give me a fucking break, she had muttered before the line went dead. *Please.*

"This is weird," Bethany said, the vague language of the habitual marijuana user overtaking her vocabulary, "but I remember that! I was in bed trying to read that book about the church again, and I had made it to Chapter 3, 'Freedom Bound by Love,' or whatever. Bobby was down in the garage looking at his porno magazines with Devon, and the phone rang, so I picked it up without thinking—"

"And there I was," Thomas interrupted, continuing to knead her neck muscles, "your favorite heavy breather."

"You were not!"

"Well, I was breathing at least."

Bethany threw her head forward and sighed. "I *wish* you had made an obscene phone call," she said. "I mean, I had this inkling that it was you, but how could I ever get that verified? I tried to star-69 you, and the recorded voice said something about an unavailable or private line. So rude that lady!"

"The number at the parsonage is known," he explained, "but not listed in any directory."

"Like your beloved Jesus," she remarked, knowing full well that Thomas disliked unserious talk about his religion, and wouldn't take her bait. His fingers released their pressure for a moment, and just as she was about to apologize they found another knot, encircled it, and pressed down hard. "That's perfect," she said, arching her back in exquisite pain. "Please don't stop . . ."

And then he had told her: "We should really speak about the state of your marriage, Bethany."

"Oh, I don't want to! Not today!"

"An open dialogue is healthy—"

"But I'm so tired of it!"

"Another day, then?"

"Press harder," she said.

"You know I'm here whenever you're ready . . ."

"Just the back rub, please."

It was through sheer dumb luck that they had ever consummated their relationship in the first place. Bethany had been involved in awkward courtships before, but nothing touched her experience with Thomas, who, with his divided loyalties (her soul, her body), brought ambivalence to a new level altogether. Perhaps this was correct: Bethany was a married woman, after all, and Thomas was her *minister*, albeit on a trial basis, and neither of them had any practice as a sexual predator (like Allen Weinglass, for instance). Thomas would tell her, and it would come as no surprise, that he had resolved to keep his feelings a secret from her, and tried to *sublimate* his love so that it might better fuel his work as a pastor, but it didn't work! Every time he saw her in the church he felt as if he might break in two, and his thoughts, at the pulpit, were often interrupted by his terrible dilemma: whether to reveal his love to her, which was wrong, not to mention hopeless, or to keep his love a secret, which was right, but hopeless in a host of other ways (did his devotion to God preclude an earthly love? Should he reject the world of the senses like a Manichaean? According to Spinoza, wasn't all love directed toward the Ultimate Being? His love for God was not, by definition, bodily, and this had never been a problem until he first set eyes on Bethany, when his cosmology began to change: like Freud's patients in "The Most Prevalent Form of Degradation in Erotic Life," who were impotent with their wives but virile with their mistresses, Thomas felt no desire where he loved [God], and could not love where he desired [Bethany], and without some form of resolution, and soon, he feared the uncertainty might swallow him). So he decided to tell her everything at the right time, but wound up avoiding her when faced with an opportunity. The way her daughter clung to her, and stood up in the pew to whisper in her ear; and the way her son, so evidently bored with religion, slouched beside her with a blank expression, pretending that his mother, and his sister, meant nothing to him . . . And Thomas, to compound his own difficulty, refused to ask for guidance when he prayed, as he did at regular intervals throughout the day—before each meal, between appointments, whenever he found himself alone and in need of some *critical distance* from experience. Prayer was not the proper place for selfish thoughts, and his attraction to Bethany Caruso, as he saw it, was selfish to its core, not a blessed thing, a continual act of dishonesty and therefore *beneath them*, even as he measured the potential of their love, which was considerable, and fantasized about their sex life, which, as he would soon find out, was usually rushed, often sublime, and always sincere. Of course Thomas had been in love before, or at least he had thought so, but his prior relationships with women had been based on such a deep misunderstanding that he felt as if he had been single all his life, and sexually—as a younger man he'd suffered from endurance problems, and had grown used to disappointing lovers with his lack of confidence, and then listening, in an unfamiliar bed (or cringing in his own), to tender reassurances that sex was just a *thing*, when he knew from experience that, actually, its importance could not be overstated, only misunderstood, too readily accepted, confused with intimacy, &c. The mythology that black men were somehow naturally skilled at lovemaking still persisted, and the fact that Thomas was merely average in bed, or even less than so, seemed a great disappointment to women. All this would change with Bethany Caruso, his first genuine *lover*, whose reciprocal feelings brought out something chemical in him that cured his overeagerness and opened his imagination to acts of intimacy that he never would have considered without her influence, without her body as a foil for his descent into adultery.

Their stroke of good luck? Bobby, having just negotiated his way back into the marital bedroom following a stint above the garage, planned to celebrate his "exile's return" with a romantic weekend at home and had arranged for his parents to take the children. Meanwhile, Bethany had been trying to schedule a pastoral visit to the house (unbeknownst to her husband), and the only evening Thomas could spare fell on the Friday of their reunion weekend. Bobby had been furious! A quiet dinner with the pastor of her church, he believed, would have set an entirely wholesome precedent! And a stranger to boot! He could see it clearly: They would all three bow their heads and say Grace before the supper, holding hands in *love* and *chastity*, when Bobby, thinking ahead, had already purchased the safest and least invasive vibrator on the marital-aid market, hoping to revive Bethany's interest in her sexuality . . . At any rate Bobby had been summoned without notice to Davenport, Iowa, where the company needed his management skills to solve a "glitch" in the chain of command at one of their subsidiaries, and it looked as if he would have to stay until the following Tuesday, Wednesday at the latest. (But what about the special vibrator? The unveiling ceremony Bobby had imagined would never quite take place, and after six frustrating months he returned the package by UPS for a full refund.) Before she allowed herself to celebrate, Bethany made sure her in-laws would still be taking the children for the weekend. Oh, yes, Bobby's mother told her on the phone, the insipid theme song to *Entertainment*

Tonight blaring in the background, they were so looking forward to spending "quality time" with the grandkids. Which meant another trip to see Old Ironsides, because Bobby's parents were strangely obsessed with the Tall Ships. Bethany poured herself an extra glass of wine the night before, nervous and surprised that the stage for her seduction of Thomas had finally been prepared. At the office on Friday she couldn't concentrate, and spent most of her time trying to decide what to make for dinner, settling on a pasta recipe that she vaguely remembered seeing on the Food Channel. But she couldn't find all the right ingredients at the Bread & Circus, and the checkout aisles at five-thirty were a mess; and she let the vegetables overcook while she was upstairs wrestling with the zipper of a dress that made her thighs look chunky anyway, plus she wanted to seem casual, so she changed into a blouse and her favorite wide-legged slacks; and she had been lucky to hear the doorbell the first time it rang, on her way downstairs from the attic, where she had gone to find an old pair of slutty leather heels.

"I'm coming!" she yelled despite the fact that Thomas wouldn't hear her, carrying the heels in one hand and rushing, shoeless, down the staircase, a disturbing silence emanating from the kitchen, the evidence of her family, she realized much too late (winter jackets, stray gloves, a backpack), scattered everywhere.

"Just one second!"

Finally she kicked aside Jessie's bright pink snowsuit and opened the door, too frantic to worry about what she might say, how to explain the fact that they would be alone for dinner on a Friday night, when Thomas—ever wary of the unethical and the unseemly—had expected to visit with the entire family. The pastor had overdressed for the weather, wrapping himself in a greatcoat and woolen scarf despite the fact that it had been a mild February throughout New England. She invited him inside with an apology and immediately blurted out the fact that her family had abandoned them.

"I hope that's okay," she told him, tossing her pumps in the front-hall closet because she had decided against them. "There!" Bethany directed him to the coatrack and ran off to the kitchen, trying to rescue their dinner from oblivion.

Thomas would remember being left alone in the front hallway, his own heart racing with the night's potential, nearly tripping over Jessie's snowsuit, so small and pink that it reminded him of his great responsibility, and killed, for the moment, any desire he felt for Bethany. *I will live through this*, he told himself, following her through the unfamiliar rooms and into the modish kitchen, where he found her struggling to open a bottle of wine between her knees. *Here*, he said, *let me give it a whack*. Saved by the tickling of his small-talk gene! Thomas's arrival at the Pilgrims' Church had coincided with a flurry of dinner invitations, and though the congregation was relatively small, it had taken Thomas the better part of a year to visit every parishioner's home at least once, from the Angelises' mansion rising conspicuously from the stone peak of Cliff Estates, to the Swensons' modest compound just next door to Bethany (fueled in part by solar panels and heated, in the winter, by firewood), to the elder widow Margit Parmelee's one-bedroom efficiency in Kensington Meadows, the assisted-living facility just a stone's throw from Naumatuk Middle School. Slowly, with each pastoral visit, a context began to form around the faces turned so eagerly to him at the pulpit, and Thomas had gained a provisional sense of what the members of his congregation brought to worship every Sunday—just what, exactly, they kept private, choosing to confront without his help, and what they would entrust to him as their minister and *concertmaster*, as the Book of Worship put it. The range of his experience as a dinner guest was astonishing! In the unfinished baronial splendor of the Angelises' dining room, her husband working late and the children bouncing off the walls downstairs in the "rec room," Artemesia Angelis had confessed to being suicidal as a teenager, and, between dinner courses, had rolled up her sleeves to show him the areas on her forearms where she had deliberately cut herself with a razor. "Oh, well," Artemesia had sighed, "now you know my secret," and politely changed the subject to a novel she had just read by Harper Lee. After that night Artemesia had approached him with a certain shyness, and though their relations, in general, could have been characterized as cordial but distant, Thomas had often been aware of something *unspoken* between them, a bond that required no language to make it real, just a glance across the aisle, a shared feeling when he repeated the Call to the Supper: *The gifts of God for the people of God. Come, for all things are ready.*

Dinner with the Swenson family, on the other hand, had been rather hectic: first they had all donned matching rubber boots (Piotr kept an extra pair around for house guests) and carried firewood indoors from the shed; then, while the children set the table with a ruckus, Piotr had taken Thomas on a tour of the grounds, pointing out the sites where he planned to build a sauna, and an artificial bog for growing cranberries, and a pen for keeping sheep; soon Ulla had called them inside with the dinner bell, and the family crowded around the table for a feast of venison, stewed kale, and homegrown parsnips. Dag, the family Newfoundland, had taken a *special liking* to Thomas, and barked whenever he made a sudden move or opened his mouth to speak. Finally they had dragged the beast outdoors, and Thomas, beyond the point of hunger, had been able to breathe freely. After the unsatisfying dinner Piotr had brought out his "Jew's harp" for a short demonstration, to be joined by Bernie on his penny whistle, and Elka with her "fiddle," and little Pele on his toy recorder . . . Perhaps the dandelion wine had gone to his head, but Thomas seemed to remember Ulla serenading him, as Dag barked away outside the frost-covered windows, with her favorites from the Woody Guthrie songbook.

More often Thomas's pastoral visits were bittersweet, like his dinner with the elder widow Margit Parmelee, blind from cataracts and suffering from dementia, who had confided to Thomas over egg-salad sandwiches (served by an expressionless home health care worker) that she was planning to retire from Congress, and wondered aloud if the Speaker of the House, Mr. Tip O'Neill, would be disappointed in her decision. Mrs. Parmelee's husband had, in fact, represented their district in Congress for over twenty years before passing away suddenly during a committee meeting around the time of Watergate. As a boy Thomas had watched the news reports about Representative Parmelee's funeral, and he still remembered the solemnity of the Marine Guard as they gave their twenty-one-gun salute.

It was perhaps inevitable that there should have been some misunderstandings too: Take his early invitation, many times rescheduled at her own request, to have dinner with the indomitable Margaret Howard, her husband, Jerry, a virtual mute, and her disappointment of a son, Bradley, alleged to be the village drug dealer. The evening had started pleasantly enough, with cocktails and hors d'oeuvres in the sunken living room, a guided tour of Margaret's perennial beds, which she obviously took great pride in, and a helpful discussion about the strengths and weaknesses of the various church committees, but a certain *odor* coming from the kitchen—a sickly, unmistakable combination of smells—had registered with Thomas on the way back from the flower garden and soon became a distraction, compounded by Bradley's late arrival on two rumbling wheels, his unapologetic stupidity, clammy handshake, and stink of motor oil and unwashed laundry; and by the way his father, Jerry, the picture of vanished self-confidence and charm, seemed held together by pomade, a suntan, and a thick gold chain around each wrist. Thomas had hoped and hoped that it wasn't true, wanted *so much* to be mistaken, yet when the time came to sit down for dinner, Margaret had disappeared for a moment and then, with some fanfare, laid out the very spread that he had been dreading: fried chicken, stewed greens, biscuits, and white gravy. A moment passed, and then another; time had slipped its bearings, spun for a while, and then lurched forward to resume its fearful pace.

"Not so bad," Bradley said, adding for the pastor's benefit, "Thanks, Ma."

"Pretty good," Jerry chimed in. "No complaints."

"Let it never be said," Margaret spoke up, "that our village can't roll out the red carpet for a new neighbor. I'm just sorry that we couldn't square our schedules any earlier, what with my workload at the office . . . Not hungry?" she asked Thomas, finally noticing his reluctance to address the meal heaped on his plate.

"Forgive me," he said, "but my appetite . . ."

"Are you unwell?"

"Yes—"

"Well, what is it?"

"I mean, no, not unwell exactly—"

They stared.

"What I mean to say," he resumed with more composure, "is that I've always found Southern cooking to be very heavy . . ."

"Well, then," Margaret said, "that's just more in the larder for Jerry. It's his favorite meal, you know."

"Oh, is it?"

"Yessir," he chimed in again.

She leaned in close to the pastor. "I try to make it for him every Thursday. You'd think he might get sick of it after all these years . . ."

"That true, Pop?"

"What?"

"You getting sick of this?"

"Nope."

"Coolness."

"Bradley!"

"What?"

"Not at my table, understood?" She went on, "The pastor and I have church business to discuss, so if you'll kindly put a lid on it."

"You're very good to do this," Thomas offered, to break his silence, "a busy woman like yourself . . ."

"I take great pride in my family," she said, admiring her men as they attacked her dinner. "If not me, as the saying goes, who will?"

And now Thomas found himself alone—all alone—with Bethany Caruso, the only woman in the congregation he found truly fascinating, and she had opened a bottle of Pinot Noir, pouring him a healthy glass in the kitchen and leading him, bottle in hand, to the sitting room, where she cleared away the magazines and video-game cartridges from the coffee table and asked him to sit down, running her fingers through that hair of hers, and flashing him a look of such a sultry nature that he

122

wondered, really wondered, if all of this was really happening.

"Watch the Nintendo thing," she warned him, just before he tripped over a bundle of wires leading to the game console. "It's an obstacle course in here."

Thomas stepped over the machine and joined her on the couch, keeping a buffer zone of empty space between them, forced into an awkward reclining position by the sofa cushions. He could barely reach the coffee table to rest his glass of wine on a copy of *WWF* magazine. "So the nest is empty," he observed, feeling the force of gravity begin to work against him.

"Right," she answered, "except they always leave their junk behind. Just look at the mess in here." Bethany knew full well the stupefying power of the family couch and chose to stay alert by sitting on the edge of her cushion. The thing was like a country of its own! Every now and then she gave in to the sofa's consoling grip and lost herself in an episode of *Biography* on A&E. "You bring this stuff into your house and it just seems to multiply. I honestly don't know where some of it comes from . . ."

"Well," he began, about to launch into his spiel about the various excesses of the marketplace and the failure of late-century capitalism to address the spiritual needs of the same consumers it enslaved to the ideal of prosperity, when Bethany, sensing something along these lines, interrupted him, "And we don't use any of it!"

Thomas felt his willpower draining into the couch. He could no longer reach his glass of wine or make his legs move on command, yet he was visited by a strange serenity. "Sometimes I wonder if we aren't addicted to the freedom of choice."

"Are you super hungry?"

"Oh, just regular."

She handed him his glass of wine. "That's good news, because our dinner isn't turning out so well." She took a long sip from her Pinot Noir, noticed that Thomas was watching her, and told him, "You might as well know right now that my addiction to alcohol is *off-limits*. I never discuss it with anyone and I intend to keep it."

Thomas raised his hands in a gesture of innocence. "I'm not here to judge you, Bethany. I've always believed that God provided us with wine to *gladden the human heart*, as the 104th Psalm reads. The real question is: Why are you looking for joy in a bottle?"

"It's not a crutch! Did you know they say a glass of wine is good for the digestion? Or is it heart disease? Anyway, if a *single* glass is good for you, shouldn't five be even better?"

"If it helps," Thomas reassured her, "think of this as a purely social visit. There's no need to be defensive."

"I'm sorry," she said, reaching for her wine again, "it's just that having you over makes me, well, nervous. When I was a girl, the Rector of our church came over for dinner exactly once. My parents were having trouble with their marriage, and as a last resort, I guess, they invited him over to observe the family dynamic and lead us all in prayer. Talk about looking for joy in a bottle! Our Rector was a famous drunk, and after polishing off a carafe of Burgundy by himself he *commanded* us to kneel on the carpet and beg for His forgiveness; meanwhile the Rector kept his seat at the dinner table and proceeded to inhale the better part of a roast . . ."

"It's the *arrogance* of the Episcopal clergy that I find so shocking. Imagine the *pride* of that man—"

"He was a drunk! Anyway, my father ended up moving out that weekend and we all survived the split. Divorce is not the end of the world, you know, and my parents just . . . moved on." Bethany eased herself back from the edge of the couch and waited for the warmth of the cushions to envelop her. "I hear you're in great demand as a dinner guest, Thomas."

"Who told you that?"

"Oh, the whispers . . ."

"Well, the sad fact is I never learned to cook for myself, even when I was in divinity school, and it's an important facet of my job here that I make the rounds. Although I do, you might like to know, have a very strict 'no kneeling' policy—"

"That's a shame," she ventured, diverting her eyes.

"What?"

"I wonder," she went on, "who's the best cook in all the church, Thomas?"

"Well, I'd have to reflect on that."

"What I mean to say is," she tried again, rephrasing her question to sound more suggestive, "where on your pastoral rounds have you been served with the most *generosity?*" While Thomas stumbled through a diplomatic answer about the quality of the dinner conversation and the graciousness of the church membership, Bethany inched herself closer to him on the couch—without detection, she thought—and performed her most elaborate hair flip. She waited, but her approach seemed to have no effect. *How does this work again?* she wondered, still watching him, only half listening, now, as he described Alessandra Palacios y Rio's five-course dinner, which began with lobster bisque, and then she brought him a risotto of some sort, followed by—

"Sounds catered to me," she interrupted.

"Yes, I suppose it was. I'm not a food person," he admitted, "so the effort was wasted. My lifestyle is very simple."

But he looked so delicious! Normally she didn't think this way, reduce people and their personalities to morsels for her private consumption, but for once they were all alone, and she was *lonely*, in need of loving, touching, whispering, holding, and—dare she imagine it?—some religious fucking, if only Thomas would forget about his *simple lifestyle* and make a move across the sofa! By now the children would be watching, for the eleventh time, their grandparents' home video of the Tall Ships parade, complete with amateur narration ("Don't look now, but here comes the *Harvey Gamage*! Hailing from South Bristol, Maine! Hard to believe that she was built from a traditional schooner design in 1973 . . ."), and Bobby, having just availed himself of some all-you-can-eat buffet in deepest Iowa, would be setting out in his rental car to find the nearest Adult Video store, where he would scour the shelves for a starlet that reminded him of Bethany; and here she was, languishing untouched beside her favorite minister, trying to seduce him and failing miserably! It was just her luck to fall in love with the pastor of a Congregational church, who, though single, would never violate the sanctity of a marriage vow and the trust of his parishioners, even if he loved her back, not that he could, not that he ever, ever would . . .

After her second hair flip failed to get a rise from Thomas, and the pastor, by the looks of it, seemed to be fighting off the urge to sleep, Bethany suggested they move into the kitchen. Truthfully she had given up on him, and served her seduction dinner with a heavy heart. She continued to talk easily with the pastor, smiled at the right places, even laughed once or twice, but his presence seemed hopelessly benign—right down to his flannel shirt, wide-wale corduroys, and sensible leather shoes. Thomas looked handsome in the candlelight, if vaguely troubled, hardly touching his second glass of wine, avoiding her eyes and turning the subject—when he spoke at all—to church-related business. He did compliment Bethany on her cooking and admired her choice of beeswax candles, which burned, he

suggested, with a gentle light. *He's a eunuch!* she thought, longing to open a second bottle of the Pinot Noir, but resisting for
now, especially after giving that stupid speech about addiction.
Then Thomas asked about her experience as someone returning
to Christianity, and she answered him honestly, voicing her
reservations about religion in general and the Christian tradition in specific: the lack of respect for other belief systems,
which, under God, must have been equally valid; the quick fix
promised by so many followers of Jesus Christ; and, on a more
practical level, the time commitment of joining a church, which
she knew to be considerable. Thomas answered with a pitch
about the democratic aspects of the Congregational Way, and
his own belief (here she smiled to herself, realizing that she had
reached him) that religion was not about inherited ritual or tradition but *love in the here and now,* love for the Son of Man,
first, who died for our sins, love for each other, and obedience
to the Holy Spirit, which was love distilled, and the graceful acceptance of difference, including the variations of belief, because Christ taught, and His children must practice, a doctrine
of *acceptance,* and the Congregational Church, the pastor insisted, as the only church He ruled with absolute authority, had
a mandate to accept His children, all of them, no matter what
stage they had reached on their "spiritual journey." This last
phrase made Bethany wince.

"Thomas," she told him, "you don't have to talk that way
to me, not when we're alone like this. I mean, there's candles
burning. We're in the kitchen."

The pastor seemed taken aback. "I'm not sure I . . ."

"Who do you think I am? *How* could you say that to me?"

"I don't understand," he said simply. "Tell me how I'm supposed to talk to you. Please."

"Like a human being! I'll allow you that I'm not a great student of theology, but when someone casually informs me that I'm on a *spiritual journey* I have a hard time keeping a straight face. Frankly you're above that kind of thing. I don't think twice when I hear the others talking about my *spiritual journey*, but you of all people!"

"Bethany, I appreciate what you're saying, but—"

"Does my journey begin at the Burlington Mall or over at the Pier One Imports? Or in the parking lot outside my office building? Did you know, Thomas, that the company I work for makes, among many other overpriced consumer goods, satellite-guided *missiles*? Half the people in this quaint New England village work for an arms manufacturer, including myself and my dear husband, so forgive me if I'm not ready to explore my *spirituality* to its fullest."

"Yes, but—"

"And the journey itself! I wonder if my neighbors realize that their little trip to *Heaven* might not go off so smoothly as their last vacation at Sugarbush. The car's all packed and the house alarm is set and the kids are in back fighting over the Game Boy in their mittens . . . What will they say when they realize the *end is near*? Who will they call first, their team of lawyers? Their broker? What will they do when they find out their *spiritual journey* has been taking them in the *wrong direction*?" Bethany, to her own surprise, had been fighting off tears throughout, and with this last observation she began to cry— but only for a moment, and without the wailing and sobbing that sometimes reduced her to a puddle of nerves.

After a long silence Thomas said, "I'm sorry, Bethany."

"You have nothing to be sorry about," she answered, still in shock from her unexpected outburst. She wiped her face dry with a paper napkin. "I'm the lunatic at this dinner table."

"You spoke your mind," he told her with some reverence, "and I appreciate that. So few people bother with me . . ."

"And blew out a candle in the process," she observed, watching the single beeswax candle burn. "I'm glad that's over. *Phew.*"

Perhaps it was a residual effect of their argument, or the fact that, after surviving an uncomfortable hour, they were beginning to warm to each other's company, or perhaps the mention of *love in the here and now*, forgotten during her outburst, had freed their deeper motives from shyness and hesitation, because, at that moment, they began to act as if some foreknowledge had brought them together on this very night, for the sole purpose of coming together, freed from the constraints of moral agency, and Bethany, for one, would not let this opportunity escape them. "Drink your wine," she instructed Thomas, and in his own good time he would, watching as she tied her hair into a twist, held it behind her head, and let it slowly unravel on her shoulder, shining with an incandescence that outmeasured his capacity for language, that would quiet his urge to describe her the next day, when he wrote in his journal, *I looked at Bethany and forgot myself. Already she is everything*, and this realization, paired with an overheated caution about being found out, would compel him to throw not just that day's entry but his *entire journal* in the kitchen rubbish. For her part Bethany was picturing her bedroom upstairs, which she had prepared in a fit of optimism; earlier she had vacuumed the carpet free of Bobby's footsteps, drawn the window treatments for privacy, set the thermostat to a comfortable 68°, turned out the overhead light and aimed her reading lamp directly at the king-sized bed, made with her best linens—the marital suite so precious to her husband (and the builders) was in perfect shape to be defiled, and if Thomas, at the threshold, even thought of backing out, she would let it drop about the French embroidered underwear. But there was no call for such drastic measures. Thomas, who was not usually prone to explicit sexual fantasy, had been unable, for months, to stop imagining their first encounter in some detail, and while he did manage to govern his daydreams inside the Pilgrims' Church, where the Puritan saints ruled more sternly, even, than Christ himself, an image of her trailed him on his daily rounds, reminding him, as he climbed into his Ford Probe for another hospital trip, that in his heart he was a *sinner*, born from his parents' love for each other and from their brave idealism, yes, but also from *lust* and *human vulnerability*. Bethany was not to blame! He was fascinated by her beauty, her intelligence, her frustrated ambition, and though she may have tempted him to act (that tank top she had worn to an unnaturally hot Autumn Fest, the phone calls after hours, the urgent dinner invitation), final responsibility for breaking the church covenant rested, Thomas believed, with him alone. He had found no cure for his attraction, not through reading, prayer, and other religious exercises; nor would he find relief in friendly contact, private consultation, or—and this was the lowest—the practice of *onanism*, because he fantasized about her most vividly in the parsonage, when, following another night of work, he climbed the creaking staircase, undressed in silence, and prepared himself for bed, laboring under the weight of his loneliness, his old familiar loneliness, which had always, until now, provided *comfort* in his chilly bedroom, and he was always *cold*, no matter what the season, shivering alone in that drafty room, the covers piled high, the space heater humming and clicking . . . Was it sinful to imagine her with great affection on those nights? To share a pillow and feel her bodily warmth, to laugh as her imaginary double rolled on top of him? Oh, but she tormented the pastor in the a.m., finding him in the crawl space between dreaming and reality, seeming to be so material, and so intent on making love, and again, and again . . . What about the actual seduction? Bethany, in fact, was much less of a romantic by nature, and even though she (arguably) had more at stake in the affair—more to lose, she believed, while Thomas didn't bother with such calculations— she chose the right moment to approach him: they had finished all the wine in the house, hashing out their religious differences until 1 a.m.; they had just traded deep, end-of-the-week yawns across the kitchen table, and Bethany, feeling drunk and weary enough to do something *really bold*, had suggested to the pastor that their night, so long delayed, had reached an end. "I'm wrecked," she had claimed. "Let me see you to the door." She thanked him for his indulgence and advice in the gloom of the front hallway, and stood nearby while he draped himself, once again, in his protective winter clothing. (Bobby had just placed his last call to her from Iowa, but she had foreseen his concern and turned off the ringing function on all the telephones. *Call me in the morning*, he left on the voice mail, *or I'll start to worry, okay?*) Thomas was certain that their night would end in sorrow! That he would drive back to the parsonage drunk on wine and *heartbroken*, wrestling with what he might have done to change the evening's course, the charm he might have summoned from—where?—to make her laugh *at least once*, and replaying the moment, in candlelight, when he should have confessed his love and risked offending a married woman for the chance, the slightest chance, that she had prepared a confession of her own. In his mind he was already following the dark road home, past the horse farm, the high school, the nursery, the Public Works garage, and heading into Old Town, but then Bethany, taking some initiative (she knew he never would) approached him from his blind side, grabbed the lapels of his greatcoat, pushed him back against the wall, and kissed him on the mouth *without apology*, holding him in place, daring him to try to resist. The pastor let himself be kissed, thinking of a line from the 106th Psalm: *And a fire was kindled in their company; the flame burned up the wicked.* She began unbuttoning his greatcoat, revealing, in a whisper, that she *wanted him*, and wanted him profoundly, not in the manner of some bored and unloved housewife looking for a thrill, because, she told him, she was *never* bored, *always* loved, and still she wanted him, *so badly, Thomas, you have no idea.* There, pinned against the wall, his eyes half closed and his coat half open, the pastor answered, *I do.*

Second Part

7

With still no word from the pastor by noontime on Wednesday and not a sign of him emanating from the parsonage, the Reverend Kate Moore, assistant minister of the Pilgrims' Church and acting chairperson of God Loves Animals, Inc., an experimental hospice program for ailing pets, after consulting the congregation's part-time secretary, Mrs. Safarian, about the vagaries of Thomas's schedule, made the drastic step of calling Caroline Abbey, the youngest of the elder widows, to begin spreading word of the pastor's disappearance over the Pilgrim Prayerline. Mrs. Abbey was home to take Kate's first call, in fact she rarely left her house at all, ever since the Bridge Club had fallen into disarray and the nice checkout girl at Stop & Shop had told her about the home delivery service for Seniors, which she swore by, even if the boy who brought her packages was surly and ungrateful for his weekly tip, a brand-new dollar bill. Mrs. Abbey's phone had become a mostly inert object in recent years, ringing only with bad news and telemarketers (they were always trying to fleece her out of something), and she received Kate's message about the pastor's disappearance with some distress but total comprehension, taking Kate's dictation, by reflex, in Gregg shorthand, which she had last used professionally in 1972:

Mrs. Abbey relished the chance to play a role in something— anything—other than a game of bridge, and after hanging up she consulted her phone list, sealed in a plastic sleeve and stored with her bills and winter gloves in the top drawer of her dresser in the front hallway. The name just below her own on the Prayerline was Alma Acevedo, and she dialed Alma's number with a sense of urgency. The Acevedo woman she hardly knew, only that, like most females of Spanish ancestry, she was

*Pray for our pastor Thomas Mosher, who has been missing since Sunday afternoon. If you have any information about his whereabouts, please call Kate Moore immediately. We pray for the well-being of Thomas and the swift resolution of this mystery. May the Lord help us walk together in His ways as we follow the life and example of Jesus Christ. Amen.